"WILL IT BE ME?
WILL I DIE?"

Her voice shook with fear.
"You've got to tell me!"
she screamed at the board.
"Please!"

The pointer moved slowly
to the first letter . . .
then the next,
and the next . . .

All eyes moved to one person.
Her mouth was open
and her face was filled
with horror . . .

Play the gam   if you DARE!

Carol Gorman lives in Cedar Rapids, Iowa with her husband Ed who is also a full-time writer, her son Ben, and their three cats: Tasha, Crystal, and Tess. Ms. Gorman, the author of *Chelsey and the Green-Haired Kid,* as well several other award-winning books, taught language arts for seven years before resigning to write full time.

DIE FOR ME

CAROL GORMAN

AN AVON FLARE BOOK

DIE FOR ME is an original publication of Avon Books. This work has never before appeared in book form. This work is a novel. Any similarity to actual persons or events is purely coincidental.

AVON BOOKS
A division of
The Hearst Corporation
1350 Avenue of the Americas
New York, New York 10019

Copyright © 1992 by Carol Gorman
Published by arrangement with the author
Library of Congress Catalog Card Number: 91-92462
ISBN: 0-380-76686-8
RL: 5.1

First Avon Flare Printing: July 1992

AVON FLARE TRADEMARK REG. U.S. PAT. OFF. AND IN OTHER COUNTRIES, MARCA REGISTRADA, HECHO EN U.S.A.

Printed in the U.S.A.

RA   10   9   8   7   6   5   4   3   2   1

For my dear friend, Marilyn Yeager,
with thanks for many pleasant evenings
of hot tea and good conversation

PROLOGUE

Holly Baldwin pushed open the heavy doors of the public library and stepped out into the night. She shivered and zipped up her leather jacket.

She didn't see the figure crouched in the shadows of the big lilac bush. Even if she had turned to her left and stared, she wouldn't have seen anyone hiding there. Holly had spent the evening under the bright fluorescent lights inside, and her eyes hadn't adjusted yet to the black, moonless night.

Holly took a deep breath of the crisp night air and gazed down Linn Road. It was ten o'clock and the street was deserted and quiet. It was a chilly night, much colder than usual for September. The wind snatched at her long blonde hair and whirled strands of it around her head. She adjusted the straps on her backpack, stuffed her hands into her pockets, and began her walk home.

Holly didn't see the figure move quietly out of the shadows to follow her. She had no idea she was in danger.

She was thinking about her grades.

Holly was a senior and school seemed harder this year. Here it was, only three weeks into the school year, and already she was working very hard, spend-

1

ing extra hours at the library where it was quiet. She was determined to make excellent grades in all her subjects, and the only way she knew how to get those grades was by hard work. After all, she thought ruefully, she couldn't use her "magic notebook" anymore. She'd start applying to colleges soon, and she needed that extra edge to get into the school she'd been dreaming about since junior high.

Ivy League. That was important. To her parents, her friends, herself. She intended to be in pre-law, and having gotten into a good school would certainly be important when she applied to law school. And to a law firm after college.

She smiled to herself. College was just a year away. She imagined herself at graduation from Greenwood High wearing her cap and gown, receiving her diploma. The high school orchestra would play "Pomp and Circumstance" *ad nauseum* while she and her classmates filed by. She'd be excited but sorry to leave her friends.

Holly had been in the same group of friends since elementary school. Holly, Monica, and Carmen. Holly shook her head and laughed to herself, remembering the stunts they'd pulled at Jefferson Elementary School, and here. What a threesome. Oh, sure, sometimes they had fights, like all friends did. In fact, the last run-in she'd had with—

But why think about that? It was history. Most of the time, everyone in her group got along great.

There were some fun guys, too. Kent and Tom, mostly. She'd dated Kent until they'd broken up over the summer. And Tom was always a laugh. *Tom Thumb,* Holly and her friends called him, because he was so short. He hated that nickname, which made their teasing even more fun. He gave the impression he was a goofy party guy, but he was smart—yeah, like a fox.

She crossed the street at Pritchard and turned into the alley halfway down the block.

The air smelled like autumn, crisp and smoky. Dead leaves scudded across the pavement and crunched under her feet.

When she first heard footsteps behind her, she didn't even turn around. She thought she was hearing the wind clicking the branches together over her head.

She kept walking.

Because there was no moon overhead to illuminate the alley, she had a difficult time seeing where she was walking. Other than a small light bulb burning on the side of a garage about twenty yards away, the only lights were over the streets at either end of the alley.

A dog barked in the distance.

The second time she heard the footsteps, she knew someone was behind her. She looked back over her shoulder and saw no one.

Her heart skipped a beat.

She quickened her pace, but didn't run. She reassured herself that she was just a little nervous because it was dark and she'd been reading *Macbeth*. All those witches and talk of death had unsettled her.

The footsteps were probably made by someone out walking the dog or taking out the garbage or—

The footsteps came quicker now. When she looked back again she saw a figure behind her wearing a dark-colored coat and hat pulled low. The figure's head was up, seeming to look straight at her.

Holly whirled around and began to run. Her backpack was heavy and awkward, and it jostled and slammed her on the back as she ran.

She was an athletic girl, a strong tennis player. But her breathing came hard as she ran because of the backpack's added weight. And the panic that was rising in her chest.

Her lungs burned. And she kept running.

The footsteps were slapping the pavement behind her, getting closer.

"What do you want?" she cried, still running.

Maybe it's money.

She tore the backpack from her shoulders and hurled it to the ground. And she kept running.

The figure passed the discarded backpack and kept up the chase.

Seconds after throwing off the backpack, Holly's toe caught on a stone in the alley, and she fell.

Two hands grabbed her from behind.

Holly screamed and rolled over to face her attacker. She stopped short.

"Guess who?" the figure said, and smiled.

"Wha— What are you doing here?" Holly stammered. "You scared me to death!" She jerked her arm away. "What do you want, anyway?"

"What do I want?" The figure reached into a coat pocket and pulled out a small object. "I want you to die for me, Holly."

When Holly saw the gleam of the gun's metal in the dim light, a thought flitted through her head in a millisecond. The dream of graduation, Ivy League school, and law practice would never materialize. The dream was shattered. None of that was going to happen.

None of it.

When the gun went off, the dog in the distance stopped his barking for a moment. Then he barked more urgently than ever.

CHAPTER 1

"How insensitive can you get?" Jessica Reynolds said. "I mean, Holly was killed only a month ago, and already her best friends are having a costume party! Here, zip me up, will you?"

Talley Johnson moved across Jessica's bedroom and zipped up the black witch's dress. She stepped back and gazed at her friend.

Jessica looked beautiful, even in the witch's costume. Her long blonde hair fell softly around her face and shoulders and tumbled nearly halfway down her back. At five nine she stood taller than most of the other girls, but she carried her height proudly, with her head and back straight, and she always looked people right in the eye.

"I know what you mean," Talley said, seating herself on the bed. "They don't seem to be mourning very much." She stared at Jessica's costume and smiled slyly. "At least you're wearing black."

Jessica rolled her eyes, but smiled back. "Sick joke, Talley," she said. "But seriously, don't you think it's strange that those two girls, who've been together since first grade, are partying so soon after their best friend was murdered? It's so awful! And the police don't have any suspects, and no one can figure out why such a horrible thing happened."

"Yeah," said Talley. "But I figure, hey, go with the flow. I didn't know Holly very well, and if those girls don't want to mourn, why should I?"

Jessica shook her head. "I can't help wondering what her murder was all about. I mean, *why* would someone kill her? It just doesn't make any sense!" She sighed and joined Talley on the edge of the bed. "But I know what you mean about going with the flow." She smiled sheepishly. "That group was never my favorite, but I have to admit, they've always thrown great parties. You haven't lived here long enough to have experienced one of them. Ever since about fifth grade, they've taken turns hosting huge parties celebrating either Halloween, Christmas, or the coming of spring."

"Sounds like fun," Talley said.

"You're in for a treat," Jessica said. "Just because the two remaining girls are jerks doesn't mean the party won't be fun. Especially at Monica's house. Of the three girls, her parties have always been the most memorable." She smiled. "I guess I'm really a hypocrite. I've never really *liked* any of those girls, but I've always gone to their parties. Before Brit moved, she and I went together."

"You and Brit were friends a long time, weren't you?" Talley said.

"Yeah," said Jessica. "Since kindergarten. I miss her a lot." She stared at a pattern on the rug that covered part of the hardwood floor. "She and I were never really in any special crowd. We kind of moved in and out of different crowds, depending on our moods." She looked up at Talley. "Maybe we just didn't really fit in anywhere. But it was okay, because we had each other." She grinned. "I sure am

6

glad you moved here, Talley. I was starting to get a little crazy without having a good friend to hang out with.''

"Don't mention it," Talley said, smiling with pleasure. "I'm just glad I met somebody I liked here. I was really scared at first."

"Scared?"

"I mean—nervous," Talley said. "I'd imagined this town would be filled with mean, nasty kids who wouldn't like me."

"I guess I'd be nervous, too," Jessica said sympathetically, "if I had to move to a new town."

"So these parties are pretty exclusive, aren't they?" asked Talley.

"They sure are."

Talley bowed dramatically from the bed. "I feel honored."

Jessica laughed. "You know, you really look great in that gypsy costume. I like the way you put your hair up on your head. You should wear it that way more often."

Talley smiled. "Thanks."

"Your hair and eyes are so dark, you can really pull off the gypsy look," Jessica said. She gazed admiringly at her friend. "And the tambourine is a great touch."

Talley stood up and whirled around, slapping the tambourine. "I *feel* like a gypsy in this getup."

Jessica picked up her tall witch's hat and slipped it on. She looked at her watch. "The guys should be here any minute."

"So how're things going with Kent?" Talley asked.

Jessica smiled. "I think I've been in love with Kent Andrews since we were in second grade and he offered to sharpen my pencil for me."

7

Talley nodded.

"It's been really nice this month getting close to him," Jessica said. "But I think he's still a little in love with Holly. Even though they broke up last summer, her death hit him very hard. He's really a sensitive guy. He's definitely mourning."

"How do you feel about that?" Talley asked.

"Well," Jessica said, "I guess I can handle it. After a while he should be okay. Doesn't time heal all wounds?"

"I'm not so sure about that," Talley said. She paused a moment. "What do you suppose Kent ever saw in Holly, anyway?"

Jessica shrugged. "A beautiful face, a great bod— basically, those two items."

"Yeah," Talley said with a wry smile. "What a sensitive guy."

"Well," Jessica said, "Holly was capable of being really nice. She just didn't exercise that ability very often. I think she was nice to Kent. Who knows, maybe she was mellowing."

Just then the doorbell rang.

"There they are," Jessica said. "All set?"

"Yup," Talley said.

The girls hurried out of Jessica's bedroom and down the stairs. Jessica pulled open the heavy front door.

"Hi, guys," she said. "Wow, great costumes."

Standing before her were Batman and Robin.

"I wanted to be Batman," said the boy dressed as Robin, "but Kent is taller."

Jessica laughed. Tom Finch, now Robin, was a master of the understatement. Tom stood only five feet two and was thin and wiry. Jessica knew he was self-conscious about his height. In junior high, when the rest of the guys grew taller and towered over him, Tom became the class clown, earning friends—both girls and guys—with his goofy sense of humor. His best friend, Kent Andrews, stood six feet two, and was a star football player for Greenwood High.

"All ready to go?" Jessica said.

"Sure," said Kent in his deep baritone. "Let's go."

When the four arrived the party was already in progress. The curving driveway in front of the large Colonial house was packed tightly with cars, and more lined the street in front. The drapes were open and the windows were ablaze with lights. Party-goers jammed the rooms inside.

"Wow!" Talley said.

"You ain't seen nothin' yet," Tom said, grinning. "Monica's your basic blue-ribbon witch, but she really throws great parties. She always has something special planned. Hey, Kent, remember when she had that Rites of Spring party?"

"Yeah," Kent said, smiling for the first time that night. "We all had to come wearing Greek togas. Monica had this giant pool set up and we all had to jump in with our clothes on."

"Yeah," Jessica added, laughing, "and it was about thirty-five degrees outside."

"I can't wait to see what she's got up her sleeve this time," Tom said.

"Sounds great," Talley murmured, her enthusiasm clearly fading a little.

"No, this'll be fun," Jessica said reassuringly. She linked arms, Talley on one side, Kent on the other, and they walked up the long front walk with Tom right behind.

The door was opened immediately by a beautiful girl with long brown hair. She was wearing a costume that almost wasn't there.

9

"Monica, *great* costume!" Tom said enthusiastically, looking her up and down. He faltered a moment and then blurted, "Who are you supposed to be?"

Monica shifted her weight over one hip and sighed impatiently. "Don't you ever read the Bible?" she said. "I'm *Eve!*"

"Ah, yes." Tom nodded. "Eve. I get it."

Jessica and Talley laughed. Monica rolled her eyes and opened the door wider. "Come on in," she said. "Sodas are in the kitchen, munchies are all over the place."

"Great," said Jessica. "Thanks."

Monica moved past them to greet another group of kids.

"It's all becoming clear now," Tom said, lowering his voice. "Monica had this party as an excuse to wear that costume!"

"That thought had occurred to me," Jessica said, grinning. "But I wouldn't have *dreamed* of mentioning it."

"She's got the body for it," Talley murmured.

"So I noticed," Tom said. "Rotten personality. Great bod."

The four, still standing in the foyer, looked around. Just about every possible costume was being worn that night. From where they stood, they could see a Santa Claus, a caveman, a woman snake-charmer with a live snake wrapped around her body, a scarecrow, Peter Pan, a guy dressed as a genie with phony tattoes all over his chest and back, and the Pillsbury Doughboy.

"I'm going to mingle," Tom said. He headed off by himself.

Jessica looked up at Kent. He stood still, staring off into the distance.

"Hey," she said gently. "You okay?"

Kent's head snapped back to look at Jessica. "Oh," he said. "Sure."

Jessica squeezed his hand. "Thinking of Holly, weren't you?"

Kent looked at the floor. "Yeah, I guess. She always loved these parties."

Jessica felt a painful twinge in her chest. "Come on," she said, she took his hand and led him toward the living room. "Let's see who's here. You come too, Talley."

The three moved into the crowded room.

"There's Carmen," Jessica said.

Carmen, a gorgeous redhead, was dressed as Jane from a Tarzan movie.

"They were supposed to be Holly's best friends," Kent said with a snort. "I'll bet neither of those girls—Monica *or* Carmen—has even *thought* about Holly tonight!"

Jessica tugged at Kent's arm. "Let's go get some sodas and sit down." She hated to see Kent so upset, but she had to admit that he was right. The two girls seemed to be having an awfully good time.

And wearing awfully revealing costumes.

"Hi, Jessica, Kent," said a guy dressed as Robin Hood.

"Hi, Ted," Jessica said, smiling warmly. "That's a great costume."

"Yeah," Talley said. "You look terrific."

Ted Thorson really did look good. He was a handsome senior, and the only thing about him that didn't work with his costume was a pair of glasses perched on his nose. They made him look like a preppy Robin Hood.

"Are you working in the Media Center again this year?" Jessica asked.

11

Ted nodded. "Yeah. I'm helping Mr. Landenberger put all the card files into the computer."

"That must be a big job!" Jessica said.

"It sure is," Ted said. "But it's a good experience I can add to my college resumé."

"Is Tom working with you?" Jessica said. "He's an expert in computers."

"No," said Ted. "We'd love to have his help, though."

"I'll tell him," Jessica said. "Maybe he can get some credit toward graduation." She laughed and glanced up at Kent. "Tom could use a few good marks."

"Okay, okay!" Monica suddenly shouted, jumping onto a chair and clapping her hands. "Can I have everybody's attention?"

"In that outfit?" Tom called out from across the room. "Do you think any guy here is looking at anything else?"

Everyone laughed, and Monica pretended to be embarrassed.

"Okay, this is serious, you guys," she said, laughing. "It's time for tonight's entertainment."

Everyone in the room became silent, waiting expectantly.

Monica jumped down from the chair and hurried to a desk in the corner of the room. She opened the desk and took out a long, flat box.

"*Voilà!*" she said. "A Ouija board!"

Murmurs ran through the crowd.

Kent spoke up angrily. "I should've expected this from you, Monica!"

"Yeah, don't you think a Ouija board is sort of in bad taste?" said a junior named Lucy, who was wearing a pirate costume. "I mean, because of what happened to Holly?"

Talley looked over at Jessica questioningly.

"A Ouija board is to contact the dead," Jessica explained quietly to Talley. "Supposedly, spirits of the dead speak through the board."

Talley frowned but said nothing.

Monica appeared surprised at the response from the party-goers. "But I had this all planned long before Holly was mur—" Her voice trailed off.

"And so you thought, let's go on with the show, right?" Kent's face was bright red with anger. "What a trooper."

"Well, maybe this isn't in great taste," a small dark-haired girl said, stepping forward, "but we're all here. I think Holly would've wanted us to have a good time. She loved these parties."

"Right," said Carmen. "We all loved Holly, but she's gone, and moping around won't bring her back. Come on, let's play Monica's game. It'll be fun."

Several kids nodded and a murmur of agreement moved through the crowd.

Monica, realizing that everyone was with her, even if halfheartedly, smiled with relief. "Okay, who wants to try sitting at the Ouija board?" she asked. "Up to four people can use it."

No one spoke.

Monica looked around. "Oh, come on. It's fun! I know Holly would've volunteered."

Again, silence.

"Well, okay," Carmen said, her hands on her hips, looking disgusted with the reluctant crowd. "I'll do it to get the ball rolling."

Monica looked around. "Great. Who else?" Her gaze stopped at Kent. "How about you, Kent?" she said in her most seductive voice. "Everybody agreed it was okay."

13

"No way," Kent answered, the red intensifying in his face. "I'm not having any part of this."

"Talley?" Monica said. "Will you? Please?"

Talley looked at Jessica, and Jessica gave her a nudge.

"Go ahead," she whispered.

Talley stepped up to Monica.

"Great!" Monica said. "Who else?"

"I'll do it." Tom began making his way through the crowd.

"*All right*, Tom Thumb!" Monica called out, as if she were hawking a sideshow at a carnival.

Tom rolled his eyes and flashed a dazzlingly insincere smile at her. "I hate you, Monica."

"One more?" Monica looked around.

"Why not?" said Lucy, pushing her way forward.

"Great, four will do it!" said Monica.

She brought out four folding chairs from a closet and set them up in the middle of the living room in a square arrangement so they all faced one another.

"Sit," she ordered.

Carmen, Tom, Talley, and Lucy sat in the chairs.

"Okay," Monica said, hurrying to the desk again. "Let's set the mood."

She took out two dozen candles and handed them to party-goers along with books of matches. "Light the candles and turn out the lights."

The room was suddenly dark, and a hush fell over the crowd. Within a few moments, the candles were all lit and the room was filled with tiny, flickering flames. A pale, eerie glow was cast over the room where the four sat with the Ouija board.

Jessica shivered. If any spirit *was* here, she thought, the mood was certainly right for it to speak. She maneuvered herself so she could see over the shoulders of the people in front of her.

14

"For those of you who've never seen a Ouija board," Monica said in a hushed voice, "it's like a game board that has the letters of the alphabet printed on it. It also has the words *yes* and *no* written at the top. The people using the board can contact an entity from the spirit world that might wish to communicate with them. They can ask the spirit questions and the spirit communicates using the board."

"Didn't I see this on 'Geraldo' once?" Tom said.

Everyone laughed and Monica sighed impatiently. "The mood is very important here, Tom," she said sternly.

Monica picked up a small heart-shaped piece of plastic with three tiny legs.

"This is the planchette," she said. "It has a circle cut out of the middle. If the spirit wants to answer a question with a 'yes,' the planchette will move to that word and stop with the circle directly over it.

"Okay, we'll place the board on the knees of these four people," Monica said.

Then she placed the planchette in the center of the board.

"Will each of you rest your fingertips on the top of the planchette?" Monica said. "Very lightly."

The four did as Monica instructed.

"Now you may ask if there are any spirits present," Monica said.

"Okay, I'll bite," Lucy said. "Are there any spirits here with us?"

At first nothing happened. Then the planchette began to move around the board under the fingers of the four kids.

Talley gasped. Then there were titters from the onlookers.

"One of those four is pushing it," someone said softly across the room.

15

"I'm not, I swear," Tom said, appearing surprised. "This is really weird." He looked around at the other three. "Are any of you pushing it?"

Talley, her eyes big, shook her head no.

"I'm not," Carmen said in a hushed voice.

"I'm not either," said Lucy.

"Is there a spirit here?" asked Tom.

The planchette slowly moved to the word *yes*.

A murmur ran through the crowd. Jessica felt a tingle run up her back.

Kent leaned over to Jessica. "This is a crock," he said with disgust.

Jessica didn't respond. She seemed unable to take her eyes from the four people huddled over the board.

"What is your name, spirit?" said Lucy.

The planchette paused, then moved around the board and stopped at the letter M. Then it moved directly to the letter I.

"M—I—" Tom said.

The planchette finished the name.

"Michael," said Lucy. "There's a spirit here named Michael."

"Michael," Talley repeated softly. She gazed at Jessica with fear in her eyes.

"Of course," Kent said loudly. "It would be Michael, and not some name like Elmer, or Horace, or Walter." He shook his head. "This is for idiots."

Jessica squeezed his hand, hoping he'd be quiet. She didn't think she really believed in all this, but the mood was kind of scary and fun, and she was enjoying it.

"Quiet, Kent," Monica said. "Go on. Ask Michael some questions."

"Is there something you'd like to share with us, Michael?" Lucy asked.

16

The candlelight illuminated the faces of the on-lookers. The flames flickered and caressed them. And all eyes in the room were riveted on the Ouija board.

The planchette moved to the *yes*.

"What is it?" Lucy pressed. "What do you want to tell us?"

The planchette spelled out H-O-L-L-Y M-U-R-D-E-R-E-D.

There was a gasp from the crowd.

"Oh, that's enough!" Kent cried. "What do you people think you're doing?"

Jessica put her arm around Kent's waist and held on.

Lucy didn't seem to notice Kent's outburst. "Yes," she said softly. "Holly was murdered."

M-O-R-E, the planchette spelled.

"More?" Tom said. "More what?"

The planchette began to move quickly, almost desperately, it seemed, back and forth across the board.

The room was absolutely quiet, everyone waiting to see what the spirit Michael had to say.

The planchette moved and stopped, moved and stopped.

"What's it saying?" someone asked.

The planchette stopped for the last time, and there was utter silence in the room.

Tom cleared his throat and shifted in his chair.

"What did it say?" Jessica asked finally.

Tom looked up at her and then around at the three kids sitting with him. "*More*, it said. *More will die*."

CHAPTER 2

Talley leaned her elbows on the small table in the mall courtyard and gazed at Jessica. "How long did it take for Kent to calm down last night?" she said.

"He didn't," Jessica answered, jabbing at the ice in the bottom of the Coke cup with her straw. "He fumed all the way home." She looked up at Talley. "You have to admit it—that Ouija board message was pretty spooky."

Talley shivered. "Tell me about it."

"But what was going on?" Jessica said. "I don't believe in spirits talking from the dead. At least, I don't *think* I do." She leveled her gaze at Talley. "Someone was really pushing the planchette, right?"

"I have no idea," said Talley. "I just know *I* didn't push it, and it felt as if it took on a life of its own."

"But that's *National Enquirer* stuff." Jessica waved her hand dismissively. "This spirit named Michael just *happens* to be within hearing distance of Monica's party? So he makes an appearance and announces that Holly's not the *only* person who'll be killed? It's just so hokey!"

"Yeah," Talley said. "But kind of scary."

"On the other hand, why would any of those

three—Carmen, Tom, or Lucy—decide to make the 'spirit' say that more people are going to die?" Jessica said.

"A joke?" said Talley.

"A *sick* joke," Jessica said.

"I thought it might be Tom," Talley said. "I wouldn't put it past him—"

"Yeah," Jessica said. "But Tom is Kent's best friend. He knows how upset Kent's been about Holly. He wouldn't have pulled something like that, especially not so soon after Holly's death."

Talley shrugged. "Well, I can't figure it out." She slurped up the last of the 7UP in her cup. "Want to shop some more or head for home?"

"I suppose I'd better get home," Jessica said. "I'm on my own this week, remember? Ish has to be let out every four hours or so. She's getting pretty old."

"Who named your dog Ish?" Talley asked.

"I did." Jessica grinned. "When we brought her home the first day from the animal shelter, she was just a puppy, and we couldn't figure out what breed she was. She was sort of spaniel*ish*, kind of poodle*ish*, and a little terrier*ish*. So I just called her Ish."

Talley laughed. "Where did your parents go?"

"Dad's on a business trip to Chicago," Jessica answered. "Mom went with him." She settled back in her chair. "I've always thought it'd be fun having the house all to myself, but last night, I was too nervous to enjoy it."

"Yeah," Talley said. "I double-checked the locks at the doors and windows before I went to bed. And Mom and Dad were *home*."

"Ish is a good watchdog," Jessica said. "If someone broke in, she'd jump all over him and probably

19

lick him to death, but she'd bark a lot first when she heard the noise." She looked up and spotted a face in the crowd of shoppers. "There's Monica. Let's go. I don't want her to see us."

"Where is she?" Talley asked, getting up from the table.

"Looking at the makeup just inside Stewart's Department Store," Jessica said, turning her face away. "Don't look."

"Why don't you want to talk to her?" Talley asked, her voice hushed.

The girls had to pass the entrance to Stewart's to get to the nearest exit, but they kept their heads down and hurried.

"She'll want to talk about Kent walking out of the party—" Jessica whispered.

"Oh, Jessica!" Monica called out. "Talley!"

Jessica groaned softly but turned a pleasant face toward Monica. "Hi," she said. "Great party last night, Monica."

"Sorry you two left so early," Monica said, strolling over to the girls. "Was Kent really that upset?"

"Yes, I guess he was," Jessica said.

"By a Ouija board?" Monica frowned. "It was supposed to be *fun*."

"Monica," Jessica said, "you have to admit, the message from the board was a little—unsettling. I think everyone was kind of spooked."

"Well," Monica replied, pouting, "after Kent stormed out and *you* followed, the party just wasn't the same. It really threw a damper on everything!"

Jessica didn't feel like apologizing for ruining Monica's party. After all, it was Monica's idea to have a party right after Holly's death. And it was Monica who insisted that they use the Ouija board to try and contact the dead.

"I have to be going," Jessica said. "My parents aren't home, and I need to let out the dog."

Monica rolled her eyes. "Oh, sure, Jess, go ahead and let out your dog. Don't let *me* keep you."

"Yeah, well, bye," Jessica said.

She and Talley hurried out to her old Dodge.

"What a jerk," Jessica said, starting the engine. It sputtered a little, then died. "Come on, Baby. Don't quit on me." She turned the key again and the engine roared to life. Jessica grinned. "You just have to know how to talk to her."

"Monica really *is* a creep," Talley said. "Why are all the gorgeous girls the ones with the crummy personalities?"

"I don't know," said Jessica. "I guess they get to be really popular and think they're the center of the universe." She glanced over at Talley. "At least *you* didn't turn out that way."

Talley smiled. "I'm a late bloomer. When I was in elementary school, I was really ugly."

"You're kidding!" Jessica said, pulling out of the mall parking lot. "I don't believe it."

"I looked really bad," Talley said. "Glasses, braces, no front teeth, short frizzy hair."

"No way! Really?"

"Really," Talley said.

Jessica laughed. "Well, you've made up for lost time, girl."

Talley grinned. "Thanks."

Jessica turned her car toward home.

"Are you and Kent going out tonight?" asked Talley.

"I hope so," Jessica answered. "But after last night, I don't know whether he'll be in the mood."

"I bet he's gotten over it," Talley said. "After all, it's Saturday night."

"Maybe there'll be a call from him on the answering machine when I get home," said Jessica. "I'd hoped he'd call this morning, but he didn't."

"Why don't you call him?"

"I will if I don't hear from him," Jessica said. "Want to come over for a while? Or should I drop you at your house?"

"Better drop me," Talley said. "I promised Mom I'd get the last of my boxes unpacked this weekend."

"Unpacked?" Jessica said. "You mean, from when you moved here—last June?"

Talley grinned. "I'm the world's best procrastinator."

Jessica laughed. "You're even worse than I am!"

She pulled into the Johnsons' driveway. A man wearing old tan pants and a blue work shirt was raking leaves.

"Is that your dad?" Jessica said.

"Yeah. Well, thanks for the ride."

"Sure." Jessica popped her seat belt off, and when Talley looked at her questioningly she asked, "Can I meet your dad? I still haven't met him, you know."

"Oh, sure," Talley said, "but why don't you meet him sometime when he's not in his old work clothes." She glanced back at him over her shoulder. "He might be embarrassed to meet you now."

"Well, okay," Jessica said. "But invite me over sometime. I'd really like to meet your family."

"It's just Mom and Dad and me," Talley said. "But I'll have you over real soon."

"Okay," Jessica said. "I'll hold you to it. You've met *my* family." She smiled. "You *lived* with my family for three days at the cabin on Turtle Lake!"

"Yeah," Talley said. "That was fun, even though I never did learn how to water-ski."

Talley's father put down his rake and waved at the girls. Talley got out of the car and turned to Jessica. "See you Monday, Jess."

"Right," Jessica said. "See you."

She backed out of the driveway. Talley's father strode across the yard to Talley and waved again at Jessica.

Jess waved back. "He wasn't embarrassed," she murmured. "*You* were, Talley girl."

Oh, well, she thought, I'll meet him some other time. She always liked her own parents to look good when they met her friends, too. Still, it seemed a little strange that she'd spent so much time with Talley during the last five months, but Talley had never once invited her over or introduced her parents.

She shifted into first gear and pulled away.

It was a short drive home, less than a mile down Clairmont Street and a left turn onto Fairview Drive. She drove in the driveway at the back of the house, pushed the remote-control button to open the garage door, and pulled inside.

Jessica got out of the car and heard Ish barking a greeting. She unlocked the door leading into the kitchen and Ish leaped up to greet her.

"Hey, Ish, you really are a good alarm dog, you know that?" Jessica said, ruffling the dog's furry neck. Ish *woofed* softly, excited to see her. "You want to go outside?"

Ish, hearing the word she understood, began dancing happily around the vinyl floor. Jessica patted the dog's head and led her across the kitchen to the back door. She opened the door and Ish pranced into the fenced-in yard.

She checked the answering machine in the living room and found the red light flashing. One message had been left.

"Good," she mumbled, and pressed the play button. Maybe Kent was feeling better and in the mood to go out.

"Hi, dear," came her mother's voice from the machine. Jessica felt a small pang of disappointment, but settled down on the couch to listen. "We're having a good time in Chicago. We didn't call you last night—I remembered you had that party to go to. Anyway, we saw a play and by the time we arrived back at the hotel, it was awfully late, so I didn't want to wake you. Hope everything is fine. Remember, I left the hotel number on the pad there next to the phone if you need anything. I'll try back later. Love you. Oh, Dad is standing here blowing kisses to you. Bye, dear."

Jessica smiled and pushed the rewind button. Then she picked up the receiver and dialed Kent's number.

She heard it ring several times and then his mother answered.

"Hello?"

"Hi, Mrs. Andrews, this is Jessica."

"Oh, hello, Jessica." Mrs. Andrews sounded distracted, as always.

Probably her maid quit, Jessica thought. *Or some other catastrophic event.*

Jessica didn't care much for Kent's parents. They were big wheels in town and very social. And very rich. Jessica thought Kent's parents looked down their noses at her. And most of the rest of the town.

Kent had told her, though, that they'd *loved* Holly.

Of course. Holly's parents were also dedicated to the proposition that all people are created equal. As long as they were white males, Anglo-Saxon, Protestants. And rich.

It was a good thing Kent wasn't like that. Maybe he was adopted.

24

"Is Kent there?" Jessica asked.

"No, he's not, I'm afraid," said Mrs. Andrews. "May I take a message?"

"Yes, would you have him call me, please?"

"Certainly," Mrs. Andrews said.

Jessica wondered if he would really get the message. Half the time she asked Kent's mother to have him call her, she didn't hear from him. When she'd ask him if he'd gotten the message, he'd say something like, "Oh, yeah. I guess I forgot to call you back."

Jessica was sure he was protecting his mother.

She hung up and returned to the kitchen. She fixed herself a snack that she decided would be her supper: a chicken sandwich, an apple, and a glass of iced tea.

She ate at the dining-room table and thought about the party last night. The Ouija board's message had scared her more than she'd admitted to Talley. She didn't really believe that spirits were talking through the board last night. At least, she didn't believe it in the light of day. But what was a reasonable explanation?

Did Carmen think she could liven up the party by delivering a message that would scare everybody? Was Tom playing one of his practical jokes?

It didn't make sense.

Could the Ouija board really be an instrument to contact the dead? *Well, if that's true,* Jessica thought ruefully, *why didn't* Holly *make an appearance, since she liked those parties so much!*

Jessica wished Brit hadn't moved to the West Coast. She missed her old friend so much and felt a little adrift without her. They had exchanged a dozen letters in the first month of the summer after she'd moved, but the letters were coming less and less frequently.

Jessica sighed. She and Brit would have talked about the Ouija board for hours after the party. Brit had always helped her focus her thoughts and come to sensible conclusions.

The phone rang shrilly in the living room, and Jessica jumped up from the table and ran to the phone. Maybe it was Kent.

"Hello?"

"Jessica, it's Monica." Monica's voice sounded shrill.

"Hi, Monica." Jessica figured Monica had called to complain again about Kent's and her early departure from her party. Jessica's first impulse was to offer Monica an excuse about being busy and hang up.

But there was something urgent in Monica's voice that made Jessica pause.

"Can I come over?" Monica said, her voice half an octave higher than usual. She sounded nearly hysterical. "Right *now?* I've got to see you, Jess. It's *important!*"

CHAPTER 3

Jessica didn't finish her supper. Monica had sounded so upset, Jess lost her appetite. She wrapped up the rest of her food and put it in the refrigerator. Maybe she'd feel like eating it later.

She stood in the living room and waited for Monica, wondering what had disturbed her so much. It was probably nothing. Monica tended to get hyper about little things.

But it was, after all, only a little over a month ago that Monica's best friend had been murdered. That was certainly nothing "little." Probably, though, this had more to do with Kent's and her leaving the party early. Monica didn't take personal affronts lightly.

Monica pulled up in front of the house in her father's Buick convertible ten minutes later. Jessica watched her get out of the car and hurry up to the door.

"What's up?" Jessica asked her after pulling open the heavy front door.

"Are your parents here? Or Talley?" Monica asked abruptly.

"No, my parents are out of town for the week," Jessica said. "I took Talley home."

"Good." Monica strode past Jessica into the living room and collapsed on the couch.

Jessica, finding herself left standing in the foyer, shook her head and murmured, "Make yourself at home, Monica."

Monica had always been pretty theatrical, and tonight was no exception. She draped herself over the couch, her head resting on the back with her hair splayed out dramatically around her face.

"What's happened?" asked Jessica.

"It's happened *twice* now," Monica said. "I thought the first time was a joke, but now I know he means business."

"What are you talking about?" Jessica sat next to Monica on the couch.

"Notes," Monica told her. "Threatening notes." She pulled two folded sheets of notebook paper out of her bag and tossed them at Jessica.

Jessica unfolded one paper and started to read. Monica leaned over her shoulder.

"No, that's the second one. Read the other one first," she said.

Jessica opened the other note, obviously typed on an old, portable typewriter, and read it.

You are an evil girl, Monica. Your best friend was murdered and you don't give a damn. People like you shouldn't be allowed to exist.

Jessica looked at Monica, who was watching her carefully.

"Go ahead," Monica said, "read the second one. I just got that one this morning. I found it taped to the door when I got home from the mall. Fortunately, my parents have been car shopping all day, or they would've found it first."

Jessica opened the second note and read.

I've made my decision, Monica. You are going to die, just like Holly. She was an evil girl, too. You won't know when it's coming. It'll be a surprise. Do you like surprises, Monica?

A shudder ran uncontrollably through Jessica's body. "Do you think these came from Holly's killer?" she asked.

"Who else would they've come from?" Monica said. She grabbed the papers out of Jessica's hand and stuffed them back into her bag.

"Don't you think you ought to take them to the police?" Jessica said. "I mean, this could be a joke, but I wouldn't take a chance that it's not."

"I don't want to talk to the police," Monica said, flinging herself back on the couch again. "At least, not yet."

"Why not?"

"Because I know who wrote them," Monica said.

"Who?"

Monica turned and looked squarely at Jessica. "Kent Andrews."

For a moment, Jessica was speechless. Then she found her tongue. "I can't believe you said that! Kent would never write you notes like that!"

"He might if he'd killed Holly," Monica said.

"What? Are you crazy?" Jessica said angrily. "Are you really accusing Kent of murdering Holly?"

"I've suspected him all along."

"That's ridiculous!" Jessica snapped. "He's very depressed about Holly's death. You saw him at your party! He was furious that you and Carmen seemed to be taking Holly's death so lightly."

"That's what I mean!" Monica said. "I think

Kent is now *sorry* about killing Holly. Now he's angry with me for having that party so soon after Holly's death.''

''That doesn't make sense! Why would Kent kill Holly?'' Jessica demanded. She could feel a hot, prickling sensation in her face and knew she must be beet-red. ''He and Holly'd just broken up. He'd *wanted* to break up with her—he told me himself!''

''Kent and Holly were always fighting,'' Monica said. ''Holly was upset all the time—angry one minute, depressed the next—because they fought so much. Kent was very jealous. You know how pretty she was! Every guy in school was hitting on her, and Kent didn't like that one bit!''

''But they'd broken up at least a month before she was killed,'' Jessica pointed out.

''So what?'' Monica shrugged. ''He was probably still mad and hurt.''

''But he *wanted* to break up with her!'' Jessica repeated.

''That's not what Holly told me,'' Monica said. ''She told me Kent begged her not to break up with him.''

''*Begged?*'' said Jessica. ''That doesn't sound like Kent. He wouldn't beg for anything.''

''Yeah, Holly said when she saw him the next day, he'd gotten hold of himself and seemed embarrassed about how he'd acted. But he was still really upset.''

''Well, I don't believe any of this,'' Jessica said firmly. ''Kent didn't send those notes to you. He *was* angry about the Ouija board, but not enough to send you threatening notes. And he's certainly not a murderer!''

''Open your eyes, Jessica,'' Monica said, her voice hushed. ''Your boyfriend's a killer. Just watch him, and see what I mean." Her eyes glazed over then and she stared into the distance over Jessica's shoulder. "I just hope Michael was wrong."

"Michael?"

"The Ouija board!" said Monica. "Michael told us there would be more murders."

"That ridiculous game of yours!" Jessica cried. She stood up. "This is just stupid, Monica. I can't believe you'd think that about Kent. You'd better go now." Monica didn't move. "Get up, Monica. You're leaving."

Monica shrugged and got up with a big sigh. Jessica ushered her to the foyer and opened the front door.

"Just don't say I never told you," Monica said before she disappeared out the door.

Jessica shut the door firmly and locked it.

She paced across the floor, replaying everything Monica had said.

Jessica had never liked Monica very much. She and Holly and Carmen had always been pretty mean to other kids. But this accusation was more than Jessica could take. It was so ridiculous! Monica, like Jessica, had known Kent since they were little kids. How could she believe him capable of killing—

It was ridiculous!

She climbed the stairs to her room and stretched out on her bed. Her stomach was upset, and she felt a little sick.

She lay there and rolled onto her side. A picture on the shelf over her desk caught her eye. She got up, moved across the room, and lifted the picture from its spot next to the music box Kent had given her for her birthday last month.

The picture had been taken in second grade. Her whole class had come to the family cabin at Turtle

Lake for a cookout. Twenty-five faces, many with toothless smiles, stared out at her. She was standing in the middle row next to Holly Baldwin.

Kent Andrews was seated in the front, cross-legged on the ground. Dressed in blue jeans and a red-and-white Cardinals T-shirt, he leaned his elbows on his knees and grinned at the camera.

Kent Andrews was the little boy who'd sharpened her pencil for her and yanked playfully on her hair when he ran by on the playground. He was the same kid who grew up and swept her off her feet.

Jessica shook her head. How could anyone think Kent was capable of killing? Kent Andrews wasn't a killer! That was *impossible*.

CHAPTER 4

By eight o'clock, Kent still hadn't called. Jessica was sure his mother hadn't delivered her message, so she called the Andrews' house again.

This time Kent answered.

"Hi, Kent." Jessica decided not to ask him if he'd received the message from his mother. He probably wouldn't tell her the truth anyway.

"Hi, Jess," he said. He sounded as distracted as his mother.

"There's a good movie at the Strand tonight," Jessica said. "You want to go? I hear it's really funny."

"Oh. Yeah, okay. I'd like to get out for a while. Yeah, a comedy sounds good."

"It starts at nine-ten," Jessica said. "You want to ask Tom? Maybe he and Talley would—"

"No," Kent said. "I'd rather just go with you. I'll pick you up in a half hour." And without another word, he hung up.

Jessica was stunned by his abruptness. She looked vacantly at the receiver in her hand and slowly set it in its cradle. She was happy that Kent wanted to be only with her tonight, but this wasn't like Kent.

Normally, he enjoyed getting together with another couple—usually Tom and his date.

She went upstairs, showered, and changed her clothes for the movie.

Kent arrived thirty minutes later. Jessica walked out to his car at the front curb and climbed into the seat beside him.

"Hi," she said.

He glanced over at her. "Hi."

"You okay?"

"Yeah," he said. But he didn't look at her. "Sure."

Jessica saw the muscles in his jaw tighten. He shoved the car into first gear and peeled away from the curb, his tires screeching loudly.

Jessica didn't say anything but turned and faced the front of the car. She had no idea what was going on.

Tugging at her from a dark corner of her mind was the conversation she'd had with Monica that afternoon. She'd shoved it out of the way, not allowing herself to think about it. But now it was beckoning to her, demanding some attention.

Was she sitting next to a killer? Kent had been acting strange since Holly's death. Jessica had attributed his behavior to a normal grief over a friend's death. But was there something more?

Had Kent really been so obsessed with Holly that her breaking up with him had driven him to murder her? Had Kent intentionally misled Jessica into believing that *he* broke up with Holly, when in fact, he'd been dumped by her? Was his constant distraction caused by anger—or guilt?

Jessica stole a sideways glance at Kent, who stared straight ahead at the road, his face a mask carved in stone. Jessica couldn't stand the silence anymore. She *needed* to talk to Kent.

"I've been thinking about Holly," she said casually. She noticed a muscle jump involuntarily on the side of Kent's face. Her stomach tightened, but she made herself continue. "Remember how, even when we were little kids, she and Monica and Carmen were inseparable?" She forced a little laugh. "They really got into a lot of scrapes."

"Yeah," Kent said.

"They weren't always the nicest kids in class," Jessica pressed on, "but things were never dull when any of them were around. Remember when they locked that girl in the custodian's closet in second grade? What was her name?" Kent didn't respond. "Oh, yeah, Susan Johnson. And remember when they had food fights in the cafeteria? And they traded identities whenever we had substitute teachers? Remember when one of the subs ended up crying and running down to the principal's office?"

Kent remained silent. Jessica didn't know what his silence meant, but continued to talk and watch his face.

"But Holly was the most beautiful of the three girls," said Jessica. "She was envied by every girl in the class. Every one of us would've traded places with her in a minute."

Kent turned to look sharply at Jessica. "You're worth a thousand Holly Baldwins."

That surprised Jessica. "You must've liked her at one time," she said. "She was your girlfriend."

"I did like her. Until I really got to know her."

"But last night at the party, I thought—" Jessica started to say.

"I don't like her friends," Kent said. "I never did. And that Ouija board thing was ridiculous!"

"Yes, I guess it was," Jessica said. She decided not to press any further.

They arrived at the movie theater a few minutes later. Jessica saw Monica and Carmen across the lobby buying popcorn, so after they'd bought their tickets, she steered Kent into the darkened theater and halfway down the aisle to seats in the middle. She didn't want to run into either of the girls.

The lights dimmed and the screen sprang to life with coming attractions. The theater filled up quickly during the trailers for upcoming movies and Jessica felt herself begin to relax.

This is what I needed, she thought. A diversion. Kent obviously needed it, too. She took hold of his hand and squeezed it. He squeezed back, but kept his gaze on the screen.

When the movie began, Jessica was drawn in immediately. The comedy featured some of her favorite actors, and Jessica became immersed in the story. It was nearly fifteen minutes before Jessica, laughing along with the rest of the audience, became aware that Kent wasn't laughing.

Had he been silent from the beginning of the movie? She couldn't remember that he'd laughed at any of the funny moments.

She glanced over at Kent. He sat stiffly beside her, watching the moving images on the screen. But his face was blank, frozen into an expressionless stare. There wasn't a sign of a smile, even though the crowd in the theater was laughing loudly.

What's on his mind? Jessica wondered. He'd been quiet during the weeks since Holly's murder; he'd certainly been upset at Monica's party and angry about the Ouija board. But now, there seemed to be something more.

What was going on?

Jessica found that she now couldn't keep her mind on the film, either. Her conversation with Monica kept creeping back into her consciousness. She felt uneasy and restless.

"Excuse me," she whispered to Kent. "I'm going to the rest room."

Kent mumbled something and turned back to the screen. She climbed over the people in her row, murmuring soft apologies, and walked hurriedly up the aisle. She crossed the lobby, walked into the rest room, and closed herself in the stall on the far end.

Just as she sat down, she heard the door open and feet shuffle in.

"What's *with* you, Carmen?"

Jessica recognized Monica's low, husky voice. Everyone thought she had a sexy voice, but right now she sounded very angry.

"The cops are still after me!" answered Carmen. "I was going to talk to you after the movie, but I can't stand to wait."

"What do you mean, the cops are after you?" Monica said.

"Detective Curry came by to talk to me again about Holly!"

"Of *course!* He's still working on the case," Monica said. "So what! He's talked to me a half dozen times, too."

"I *lied* for you, Monica!" Carmen's voice was hushed but urgent.

Jessica leaned forward to hear. She was glad she'd chosen the stall at the far end of the long room. Obviously, the girls didn't know anyone else was here.

"You did not lie!" Monica snapped.

"Well, I didn't tell the detective about that horrible fight you and Holly had the night of her death," Carmen said.

"Carmen," Monica said, "if you tell him about that fight, he'll think I killed her!"

"But he keeps asking if Holly had any arguments with her friends before she was killed," Carmen said. "And I keep saying no."

"You aren't lying," Monica said. "It wasn't a fight in the way *he* means." There was a pause. "You don't think I killed Holly, do you?"

Carmen didn't answer.

"You're not *sure?*" There was a loud bang, and Jessica realized that Monica had just slammed her hand into one of the stall doors. "Oh, that's just *great*, Carmen!" Monica yelled. "Some friend *you* are!"

"But you slapped her!" Carmen said. "Right across the mouth! I didn't think that stuff happened between friends except on soap operas."

"I can't believe you're saying this!" Monica cried.

"I just want to tell the police the truth. I don't want to lie for you anymore."

"You *can't* tell the cops about our fight!" Monica said with more ferocity than Jessica thought was possible. "They'll charge me with *murder!* I'll go to prison! That'll ruin my life, do you hear me? You can't *do* that to me!"

"I won't lie for you anymore," Carmen repeated.

"Listen," Monica said, "I'm really scared. Michael said someone else is going to die."

"You really believe that Ouija board?" Carmen said.

"I don't know. But I'm scared about those threatening notes. I'm so jumpy. I could be the next person who dies—or you."

"Me?" Carmen cried.

"I just don't need any more problems!" Monica said. "I don't want to have to worry about the cops, too. I don't need this *stress*, Carmen! Just keep your mouth shut, okay?"

"I can't," said Carmen.

"Listen, Carmen, you don't know the whole story."

"What are you talking about?"

"Holly was involved in—something," Monica said, her voice faltering.

Carmen gasped. "Drugs?"

"No, not that," Monica said quickly. "But it would've ruined her chances to get into a good school if anybody'd found out."

"What was she doing?" Carmen demanded.

Just then, the rest-room door opened and feet tromped in.

"Come on," Monica said. "I'll tell you later."

The door opened again and the two girls quickly left.

Jessica sat there, stunned. She'd just overheard a conversation that put a whole new light on Holly's death.

Monica and Holly had had a serious argument just before Holly was killed, an argument bad enough that Monica didn't want the police to know about it. But there was a new dimension to the story now. *Holly was involved in something,* Monica had said.

What was it? Was Kent involved in that something, too? Did Monica know something about Kent that Jessica didn't know? Was that why she was so sure Kent had pulled the trigger that night in the alley? Or was Monica using Kent—framing him— to camouflage her own guilt? Maybe she sent those threatening notes to *herself* so she could accuse Kent of sending them!

If only those women hadn't come in the bathroom when they did! Monica was about to tell Carmen what she knew.

Jessica had to believe that Kent was innocent. She had loved Kent since she was a little girl, and no one was going to convince her that he was capable of murder.

Jessica opened the stall door and left the rest room. She was relieved to find the lobby empty, except for a few employees cleaning up at the snack counter. Monica and Carmen had apparently gone home or back into the movie theater.

She found her aisle, climbed over the people in her row, and slipped into her seat next to Kent. She expected she'd have to come up with an explanation for being gone so long.

But Kent didn't give any sign that he'd noticed she'd come back. He continued to stare at the screen, his face blank, his mind obviously somewhere else.

CHAPTER 5

Jessica scanned the faces of people moving through the lobby after the movie but didn't see either Monica or Carmen. Kent walked along with the crowd, not looking to the left or right, apparently lost in his own thoughts.

They walked out to the parking lot, got in Kent's car, and drove to Jessica's house in silence.

The house was dark. She hadn't thought to leave a light burning inside because her parents were usually home.

Kent walked her to the front door.

"Want to come in?" she said. "I have a pizza in the freezer." She'd eaten so little for supper and nothing at the theater, and her stomach was rumbling painfully.

"No, thanks," Kent said. "I think I'll go home and get some sleep. I'm really bushed."

On an impulse, Jessica put her arms around Kent's waist and looked up at him. "Kent, you're so far away tonight. You sure you're okay?"

She felt Kent's back stiffen under her fingers. "Yeah," he said. He shook his head and stared into the distance, his hands resting on her shoulders.

"You ever think that the world is a pretty disappointing place?"

"Sometimes," Jessica answered. She lightly rubbed his back through the fabric of his shirt. "Want to talk about it?"

There was a long pause before he answered. "No," he said finally. "Not now. I gotta get going." He took his hands from her shoulders.

"Okay," Jessica said, feeling a stab of her own disappointment. She had hoped that Kent would open up to her and talk.

Inside, Ish began barking.

"Have your key?" Kent asked.

"Yeah," Jessica said, digging it out of the bottom of her purse. She slipped it into the lock, opened the front door, and turned, hoping for a good-night kiss.

"I'll see you," Kent said. And with that, he turned and headed toward the dark form of his car at the curb.

"Bye," Jessica said. A sensation of emptiness formed inside her chest. No one had ever turned away from her the way Kent had lately. She felt lonely and absolutely unable to reach him.

Jessica nudged her way inside, keeping hold of the door so Ish wouldn't run out into the front yard.

"Hi, girl," she said, patting the furry head.

Jessica flicked the light on the wall to her left and the room sprang into view. Jessica gave Ish a good scratch behind the ears, then walked into the kitchen.

A frozen pizza didn't sound very appetizing, but Jessica's stomach was loudly demanding food. She took the pizza out of the freezer and put it in the oven on a cookie sheet.

The telephone rang, and Jess picked up the receiver on the wall.

"Hello?"

"Jessica? It's Monica."

"Hi," Jessica said. Monica was the last person she wanted to talk to right now.

"You up?"

"Yeah. I just got in."

"Your parents still gone?"

"Yeah," Jessica said. "Why?"

"I've got to come over," Monica said.

"Monica, is this about Kent again? I've had enough—"

"No, no," Monica interrupted. "I'm coming over. I'm bringing Carmen with me. And Talley."

"Talley?"

"Yeah."

"Monica, it's eleven-thirty, and I—"

"I need you for something important," Monica said. "I need someone I can trust. See you in a few minutes."

Click.

What now?

Jessica wished once again that she'd heard the rest of the conversation between Monica and Carmen that started in the theater bathroom. She was sure she'd have learned some very important information about Holly—and maybe Kent.

Maybe Monica was going to share some of that news when she came over. It must be important for her to come so late.

But why did she need Carmen and Talley there, too?

Jessica checked the pizza and turned down the heat. She'd eat it after the girls left.

Monica, Carmen, and Talley arrived fifteen minutes later. Jessica glanced questioningly at Talley.

"Don't ask me," Talley said, stifling a yawn.

43

"She dragged me away from a good late-night movie on TV."

"Thank God my parents were out," Monica said. "They'd have a million questions about me going out this late."

"My mom *did* have a million questions!" said Carmen.

Monica had a paper bag under her arm. She reached into it and pulled out the Ouija board.

Talley groaned. "Are you kidding? I'm missing *Carrie* for the ghost board?"

"Ouija board," Monica corrected her.

"Monica," Jessica said, "I'm not in the mood for this. It's been a long day, and I'm tired. And hungry."

"Come on," Monica said, "I need your help! I have to find out what's going to happen!"

"Why not buy yourself a crystal ball?" Jessica said scornfully. "Then you could do your fortune-telling by yourself."

"Listen, I'm getting threatening notes," Monica said. "I'm afraid someone's going to kill me! I want to ask Michael whether I'm safe or not. *I have to know!*"

Jessica sighed. "Okay, okay," she said wearily. "Let's get this over with so we can all get to bed."

She led the way into the living room.

"Put the board on the table," she said, indicating the coffee table in front of the couch.

"It works better balanced on our knees," Monica said.

"Fine," Jessica said, waving her hand impatiently. She dragged a wing-backed chair and a wooden rocker over to the couch. Talley grabbed a chair from the dining room and set it down in front of the couch.

44

The girls sat down, facing one another.

"You have some candles?" Monica said. Jessica rolled her eyes. "Well, they set the mood!"

Jessica went into the dining room and took four votive candles and some matches from the hutch and returned to the living room.

"Want some pizza, you guys?" she said. "I'll share it with you."

"I *thought* I smelled something good," Talley said, grinning.

"No, leave it," Monica said. "We shouldn't eat when we're contacting the spirit world."

"Well, geez, it's probably been a long time since Michael ate anything," Jessica said. "I bet he'd love to join us."

Monica frowned. "We'll never contact Michael if you're going to crack jokes."

"Okay, okay," Jessica said, "just let me turn off the oven so it won't burn."

She hurried to the oven and turned off the heat, glancing wistfully at the pizza through the window in the oven. Then she returned to the living room. Monica had already pulled the coffee table away from the couch. The candles were flickering on the low table next to the girls. Monica snapped off the lamp, and shadows leaped out of every corner.

"That's better," Monica said in a hushed voice.

Carmen had been very quiet tonight. She sat wide-eyed, patiently waiting for the Ouija board session to begin.

Jessica wondered if Carmen's mood had changed because of the information Monica had shared with her after they'd left the movie theater's rest room.

Monica set the board between the four of them, resting it on their knees. Then she placed the plan-

45

chette on the board, and the girls placed their fingers lightly on top of it.

"Ready?" Monica asked.

The three other girls nodded.

The room was quiet and dark. Jessica had to admit that the candles really *did* set the mood. She was sitting in her own living room, but she felt oddly ill at ease. Maybe a spirit would jump out of a dark corner. She shivered and shook that thought from her head.

Monica closed her eyes. "Michael?" she whispered softly. "Michael? Are you there?"

Nothing happened.

"Michael?" Monica said. "I need to talk to you. Are you here with us?"

The panchette slowly began to move. It slid around the Ouija board, forming a figure-eight pattern, moving faster with every pass over the board.

A chill ran up Jessica's spine. She watched the planchette move. She was not pushing it. It felt, as Talley had described it, as if it had taken on a life of its own.

She glanced around the circle at the three other girls. All of them were watching the planchette, their eyes wide with excitement. Or was it fear?

"Michael?" Monica whispered. "Is that you?"

The planchette shot up to the *yes* in the corner of the board.

"Oh, Michael, I'm so glad you're here!" Monica said. "I need your help!"

The planchette moved off the *yes* and began moving in the figure-eight pattern again.

"He's waiting," Carmen whispered.

"I know that, Carmen!" Monica snapped. "Michael," she said, her voice suddenly quieter again, "did you know I was getting threatening notes?"

The planchette moved up to the *yes*.

"What notes?" Talley whispered.

"Shhh!" Monica whispered back. She turned her face up to address the spirit as if he were hovering over them. "I knew you'd know about them, Michael," she murmured. "Michael, I have to know if I'm safe. Are these notes just a joke?"

The planchette slid up to the *no*.

Monica gasped. "No?" she whispered. "It's not a joke?"

The planchette paused on the *no,* then left it to slide around the board again.

"What'll I do?" Monica wailed. "I don't want to die!"

The planchette continued in its aimless pattern.

"Ask it—Michael—another question." Carmen's voice shook.

"You told us at my party that 'more will die,' " Monica said. Her voice broke and she cleared her throat. *"Michael, will it be me? Will I die?"*

The planchette didn't leave its figure-eight pattern.

"Michael, will I *die?*" Monica repeated, her voice suddenly loud.

The planchette didn't respond.

"Michael, you've got to tell me!" Monica screamed at the board. *"Please!"*

The planchette moved to the C, then the A, R, M, E, N.

All eyes moved to Carmen. Her mouth was open and her face was filled with horror.

"Carmen? What about Carmen?" Monica cried.

Jessica abruptly took her hands from the Ouija board and stood up.

"What're you doing?" Carmen cried. "Sit down, Jessica! I want to know what this means!"

"Please, Jessica!" Monica pleaded.

47

Jessica reached out, her body trembling all over, and turned on the lamp next to the couch.

"No," she said. "This Ouija board thing was fun at your party, Monica, but it isn't fun now. It's scary. I don't believe it, but it's scary anyway, and I'm not going to take part in it."

"You *do* believe it, or you wouldn't be scared!" Monica said.

"We're all scared," Talley said. "I think Jessica's right. We should stop this right now. Carmen, *nobody,* living or dead, can predict when somebody will die."

Carmen started to cry. "I'm so frightened!"

Jessica put her arm around the sobbing girl. "Carmen, a piece of cardboard and a chunk of plastic can't tell you *anything!*"

"It was Michael!" Carmen whimpered.

"No, it wasn't," said Talley. "Maybe you were so afraid that, subconsciously, you pushed the planchette—"

"I didn't!" Carmen cried. "I didn't push it!"

Jessica looked helplessly at Talley. She got up and walked across the room. She switched on another lamp in the corner. Maybe, with enough lights blazing, they could calm down and look at this rationally.

"Listen," Jessica said. "It's dark, it's late, and we're tired. I'm sure that tomorrow when you wake up with the sun shining through your bedroom window, you'll feel differently. This will seem very silly."

Carmen continued to cry.

Jessica looked over at Monica. Monica sat there, watching Carmen, looking calmer than she had in several days. She didn't look afraid anymore. In fact, she appeared relieved, almost pleased.

Monica glanced up and saw Jessica watching her. Monica drew in a quick breath, then leaned over to comfort Carmen.

CHAPTER 6

The ringing telephone woke up Jessica on Sunday morning. She half-opened her eyes and fumbled for the phone next to her bed. The clock on her bedside table read 8:00 A.M.

She rolled over and held the receiver next to her ear.

"Hello?"

"Hi, Jessica, it's Mom," her mother said. "I finally caught up with you."

"Oh, hi, Mom," Jessica said sleepily.

"Sorry to awaken you, dear," her mother said, "but I figured you'd be up and out of the house soon and I'd *never* get a chance to say hello."

"Oh, that's okay."

"You getting along all right?"

"Yeah," Jessica said. "Just fine." *Aside from the fact that an old friend has accused my boyfriend of murder.*

What point would it serve to tell her mother that? Her mother had always liked Kent, but maybe she'd start having doubts about him. Then she'd worry about whether Jessica ought to be seeing him. Her mother and father would probably also never leave her alone again. And it was time she grew up, Jessica thought. Time to stand on her own two feet without her parents, without Brit, without anyone helping her.

No, Jessica decided, she'd be stupid to tell her mother what was going on with Kent, with Monica and Carmen. And with the Ouija board.

"Good, glad to hear everything's fine," her mother said. "We're having a good time. When Dad is in his meetings, I shop or take a swim in the hotel pool. Then we go out to a museum or have dinner. It's been wonderfully restful."

"Sounds nice," Jessica said.

"What've you been up to?"

"Oh," Jessica said, "Kent and I went to a movie last night."

"Sounds like fun," her mother said. "Oh, Dad says we need to go. We're having breakfast with another couple in the dining room downstairs in just a few minutes."

"Okay," Jessica said. "Have a good time."

"Thanks, we will. Sounds as if you're doing fine by yourself," her mother said. "We'll call again in a few days. But feel free to call us if you need anything. Bye, dear."

"Bye."

Jessica hung up the phone and snuggled down into the covers. She was glad she hadn't told her mother what was going on. She could handle it by herself.

Her mind turned to the events of yesterday. Monica telling her she suspected Kent of killing Holly. The vacant look in Kent's eyes, as if his mind was somewhere else. Monica, in the theater's rest room, afraid that Carmen would tell the police about her fight with Holly, then saying mysteriously that Holly was "involved" in something that might have had to do with her death. And Monica insisting that the girls consult the Ouija board about her threatening notes, but looking so relieved when "Michael" hinted that it might be Carmen who would die next.

It was all so complicated. But the most important thing to Jessica was that Kent was innocent. She was sure of it. Jessica felt a loyalty toward Kent that she'd never felt with anyone else, except maybe Brit.

It wasn't because Kent was weak or helpless or couldn't protect himself. In fact, he was a big guy, half again Jessica's size. He could hold his own anywhere, with anyone. He was not only big and strong, he was also pretty intelligent. Not a straight-A student, but he got decent grades. He was no dummy.

But there was something else. He just seemed so— *sweet* was the word that came to Jessica's mind. He cared about Holly enough to feel a certain respect for her dignity after death. The Ouija board at the party had infuriated him because it wasn't respectful to her memory.

Kent was also sweet about his mother. Even though she was preoccupied with her social life and couldn't remember to give Kent his phone messages, he still protected her when Jessica questioned him about his not phoning. He cared enough about his mother to take the blame for her.

Kent was really a very special guy. Everyone seemed to like him, and Jessica felt proud to be known as his girlfriend. She felt a need to help him and protect him in any way she could.

Jessica threw back the covers and got out of bed. She'd already decided what she'd do this morning. She'd go over to Kent's house and talk to him and tell him that whatever he was going through, she wanted to help. He didn't have to explain anything to her. She'd just tell him she'd be there for him if he needed her.

51

She wanted to let him know that she cared that much.

Jessica opened the garage door using the remote control from inside the car and turned the ignition key. The engine made a few chugging noises, then stopped.

"Come on, Baby," she coaxed the car, "be good today. Dad's car isn't here for me to borrow, remember? It's just you and me. Come on, let's try it again."

She turned the key again, and this time, the engine roared to life.

"All right, Baby!" she said. "Good. Let's go see Kent."

She backed out of the garage and headed up Fairview Drive and over to Clairmont. At the end of the street, the houses on either side of the road began to get bigger and more expensive.

Kent lived on Country Club Terrace, just a block down from his mother's home-away-from-home, the Pine Creek Country Club. Jessica saw his house at the end of the street, and saw Kent's car parked at the curb where he usually left it.

A familiar red Chevy was sitting in front of Kent's car. It was Carmen's.

What's Carmen doing here? Jessica wondered. She slowed a little as she approached the house, and she parked right behind Kent's car.

The Andrews lived in a huge Tudor house on a hill at the corner. Jessica had been inside a dozen times over the years at parties with groups of kids. But she'd never approached the house by herself, and certainly not without having been invited. The size of the house alone was intimidating, towering over her at the end of the long driveway. But she thought

52

about Kent and how distracted and upset he seemed last night, and that gave her courage to get out of her car and head up the drive.

She heard voices from the back of the garage as she neared the house. Angry voices. One of them was Kent's and the other, Carmen's.

Her first intention wasn't to eavesdrop, but as she walked nearer, she realized that maybe she'd hear some important information if she listened to what they were saying. Maybe she'd learn something that would help her deal with Kent.

Instead of walking into the garage, she stepped to the side, up next to the front door. They had been too busy arguing to see her approach.

"It was blackmail, wasn't it?" Carmen said. "Holly and that 'magic notebook' of hers! She was just *asking* for trouble! But more people don't have to die!"

"You have a lot of guts, coming over here, making that accusation!" Kent said angrily. "Get out of here! Get off my property!"

"Just quit sending those notes to Monica," said Carmen.

"I don't know what you're talking about!" Kent replied.

"Oh, come on, Kent," Carmen said impatiently. "Monica's nearly going crazy—and so am I!"

Just then the front door opened next to Jessica, and Kent's mother stood in the doorway.

"Oh," Jessica blurted out, "hi, Mrs. Andrews."

"I believe Kent's in the garage," she said without opening the screen.

"Oh, okay," Jessica said.

The voices had become silent in the garage.

Jessica stepped off the front porch and walked toward the garage.

53

Kent peered out of the open garage door.

"Jessica," he said, frowning. "What are you doing here?"

Jessica forced a smile she didn't feel and put a spring in her step.

"Hi," she said. Maybe if she acted happy to see him, he would think she hadn't heard the argument. "What're you up to today?"

"Nothing much," he said, walking toward her. He glanced self-consciously over his shoulder toward the garage.

Was Carmen going to stay hidden in the back, behind the car?

"I just had an inspiration!" Jessica said, keeping her voice light. "Want to go on a picnic? You seem so glum lately, it might be fun. I thought maybe I could pack some tuna-salad sandwiches and some fresh fruit—"

"No, I don't think so, Jess," said Kent. "I told my dad I'd rake leaves today."

"Oh," Jessica said, pretending to be disappointed that her picnic plans didn't work out. She was actually feeling great relief. Kent didn't seem to realize that she'd been there, listening to his argument with Carmen. "Okay," she said. "Well, it seemed like a good idea." She shrugged and smiled at Kent.

"Sorry," he said. "Uh, I'll call you later. Okay?"

"Sure," she said. "See you later."

She walked down the driveway, got into her car, and after giving her car a few words of encouragement, drove off down the street.

CHAPTER 7

Driving home, Jessica turned it all over in her mind. What was it Carmen had said? *It was blackmail, wasn't it?* she had said. *Holly and that "magic note-book" of hers! She was just* asking *for trouble. But more people don't have to die!*

Blackmail. Holly was blackmailing someone? Or did Carmen think *Kent* was blackmailing someone? What about a magic notebook? What was she talking about? Was Carmen accusing Kent of murdering Holly because she was blackmailing someone? Had Holly been blackmailing Kent? What could she have known about him that he wouldn't want anyone to know?

Jessica's head was spinning. All of this information didn't fit together. But obviously, there were some people who knew a whole lot more about what was going on than they were telling the police—or each other.

She was worried about Kent. She thought about him in the middle of this whole mess, unjustly accused, and thrust into a maze filled with murder and blackmail. And all because he got involved with the wrong girl.

Her heart ached for him.

She wished she could talk to Brit about it. As much as she needed to feel independent, she knew she needed another head, someone else to trade ideas with. Someone else she could trust.

Maybe Talley can help sort through this tangle of information, Jessica thought. Talley had become a good friend after she moved to Greenwood several months ago. *She hasn't known all of the people forever the way I have. Maybe she can be more objective.*

Jessica drove straight home and called Talley.

"Can you come over?" she said. "I need to talk."

"Sure." Talley laughed softly. "This sounds mysterious. Does it have anything to do with that weird ghost board?"

"The Ouija board?" Jessica said. "Yeah, it does."

"Okay. As long as I don't have to sit at that board again."

"Absolutely not," Jessica said. "I've had it up to here with Michael and his spooky predictions!"

"Me too," Talley said. "I'll be over in a few minutes."

Talley arrived twenty minutes later and the girls went up to Jessica's room. They flopped on the bed, and Jessica filled Talley in on everything: Kent's distracted behavior and the arguments she overheard at the movie theater and at Kent's house.

"*Whoa,*" said Talley. "This is getting too weird."

Jessica nodded. "I know Kent's miserable," she said. "But he doesn't know how to get out of this mess."

"I see what you mean."

"It's *Holly!*" Jessica said. "She's responsible for

56

all of this! Why did Kent get involved with her, anyway?''

"Her bod? Her great looks?" said Talley. "Isn't that what you told me the other night?''

Jessica felt her face become hot and wondered if it had been a mistake to confide in Talley. After all, Talley wasn't in love with Kent and wouldn't *know* that he was an innocent bystander.

Talley was watching Jessica's face. "I know Kent's a nice guy," she said. "It's just that so many of the kids in that crowd—''

"I know what you're going to say," Jessica interrupted. "In fact, I've felt the same way. That's why Brit and I were never really a part of that group. Holly, Monica, and Carmen have always been so— well, superficial, I guess. They only seemed to care about what people look like, how much money they have, and what kind of clothes they wear. And they've always been like that. Holly was probably the worst.''

Jessica looked up at the picture of her second-grade class, then hopped off the bed to get it. "See, we were all together, even back then." She handed the picture to Talley.

"I can't believe you kept this all these years," Talley said. "I've thrown all my elementary-school stuff away. I didn't *want* to remember it." She gazed at the picture a moment without saying anything, and Jessica thought she saw Talley's hand tremble. "Where're you?''

Jessica pointed to the little blonde girl in the second row, kneeling behind Kent.

Talley smiled. "I should've been able to pick you out. You were cute.''

"Here's Holly," Jessica said, pointing. "And Monica and Carmen. And here's little Kent.''

"Where's Tom?"

"Here. And here's the girl Holly and her friends picked on the most, standing next to Tom. Her name was Susan. I felt so sorry for her."

Talley got up and moved across the room to replace the picture on the shelf. "It's hard to believe those little kids are so messed up now."

"I was thinking that just yesterday," Jessica said.

"I wanted to ask you—" Talley hesitated. "What did you think about last night?"

"The Ouija board?"

Talley nodded. "I just don't get it. How does that thing work? I mean, do you think we're subconsciously pushing that little thing, that—what do you call it?"

"The planchette?" Jessica said.

Talley nodded.

"That's the only reasonable explanation. I guess." Jessica looked at her friend. "What do *you* think?"

"I don't know," Talley said. "Do you believe in ghosts?"

"Do you?"

"There sure have been a lot of people who've claimed to see them," Talley answered.

"And a lot of people have claimed they were abducted by UFOs, too," Jessica said.

"So you don't believe any of it?" asked Talley.

"I don't know." Jessica shuddered. "It's too scary to believe it. I don't *want* to think there was a ghost talking to us!"

"But what if there was?" Talley persisted.

"There wasn't!"

"But what if there *was?*"

Jessica thought a moment before she answered. "Then someone else is going to die," she said.

*　　*　　*

After Talley went home, the day wore on endlessly. Jessica worked on homework, played with Ish, and made chocolate-chip cookies. But always there, not far from consciousness, was the worry over Kent. It colored her mood, intruded upon her thoughts, followed her around, and hung over everything she did.

Talley hadn't been much help. She couldn't provide a magical solution that would set everything right. Jessica hadn't really expected that. And it had been good to talk it over. But she felt just as frustrated as she had been before their talk. She still didn't know what to do about Kent or how to help him.

She hoped he'd call before the end of the day. But the telephone was silent.

In the evening, she sat in front of the television and watched the images on the screen, but she couldn't concentrate on any of them. She kept thinking about Kent. And Monica, and Carmen, and Holly.

Holly seemed to have more of a hold on Kent after death than she had on him while she was alive, Jessica thought ruefully.

The news came on at ten and Jessica was still sitting, mindlessly watching. Anchorwoman Bess Hartman grimly faced the camera.

"We begin the newscast tonight with a tragic late-breaking story," she said. "Less than one hour ago, a body was discovered in a ravine at the Greenwood City Park."

Jessica, startled out of her daydream, sat up and leaned forward. Wasn't this the way Holly's death had been announced? Only it had been at the very end of the newscast. It was the next morning before everyone knew who had been murdered.

59

Bess Hartman announced that their man-on-the-scene, Richard McKenzie, was rushing to the park, and that they would have a live report later in the broadcast.

Was it happening all over again? Jessica wondered. Or was this the result of an accident? She knew the park well. The ravine was deep and dark, but a lighted walking path snaked its way through the brush. A pedestrian bridge crossed over it at its deepest point. Someone could have fallen from the bridge if they had been stupid enough—or drunk enough—to climb over the guardrail.

On the other hand, could it have been murder? Could there be a mass murderer on the loose, someone who killed at random and for no reason? Was Holly a victim of the same madman? Jessica wondered if a second murder would convince Monica that Kent wasn't involved in Holly's death.

Jessica sat in her chair and waited for the live report, her heart beating hard. It didn't come on until the newscast was nearly over.

Richard McKenzie, in his live remote, stood at the edge of the park ravine, holding his microphone. Jessica hadn't liked watching him since he reported on Holly's death, shoving a microphone in front of Holly's weeping mother after the funeral, asking her, "How are you feeling, Mrs. Baldwin?"

How did he think she was feeling?

But the look on Richard McKenzie's face tonight was different. Cynical, ambitious man-on-the-scene Richard McKenzie looked shaken.

Apparently, he had seen the body in the ravine.

Behind him in the floodlights of the television cameras, two medics carried a stretcher. A body bag, obviously containing a body, rode on top of it.

"The body was found roughly an hour ago by a

60

jogger taking the lighted trail through the ravine just under the pedestrian bridge,'' McKenzie said. ''At this point, the police don't know whether they're dealing with a tragic accident—or murder.''

Jessica watched as the stretcher was loaded into the back of an ambulance. McKenzie was still talking, but she didn't hear what he said. Her mind drifted back to Holly. This must have been like the scene in the alley the night she was killed. The ambulance, the cops, the sightseers, and television cameras.

What a zoo. Jessica glanced away, but McKenzie's voice brought her attention back to the screen.

''All we can say at this time,'' McKenzie was saying, his eyes somewhat glassy, ''is that it appears to be the body of a young woman. The victim has not been identified, and police are investigating. Back to you, Beth.''

Jessica leaned back on the couch and the realization hit her like a sledgehammer.

More will die, Michael had said.

This was it.

This was what Michael had predicted.

CHAPTER 8

The phone woke Jessica up ten minutes before her alarm went off the next morning. She had slept fitfully and her head was filled with fragments of a bad dream that the ringing phone had interrupted. She reached for the phone and picked up the receiver.

"Hello?"

"Mrs. Reynolds?" It was a man's voice.

"Uh, no," Jessica said, blinking her eyes and trying to focus her mind. "This is her daughter."

"Jessica?" the man said.

"Yes."

"Jessica, this is Detective Curry from the Greenwood Police Department."

Jessica was instantly alert. Detective Curry was the officer in charge of the investigation of Holly Baldwin's murder.

"Yes?" she said, propping herself up on one elbow.

"I'd like to come by and talk with you this morning before school, if I may."

"About the body in the ravine?" she asked.

There was a slight pause on the other end. "Yes. Did you know about that?"

"I heard about it on the news last night," she replied quickly.

"I'll be over in a half hour," Detective Curry said.

"Okay." Jessica's heart was suddenly hammering hard in her chest.

The detective had hung up before Jessica could ask him her next question. *Who* was found in the ravine last night?

She leaped out of bed and ran into the bathroom. She showered and dressed and hurried downstairs. She let Ish outside and then paced around the living room waiting for the detective to arrive.

He was punctual, arriving exactly thirty minutes later. Jessica met him at the front door. He was tall and a bit heavy, and he wore a wrinkled blue suit. She glanced at the badge he flashed at her and invited him in.

"Nice place you have here," he said, looking around him.

"Thank you," Jessica said.

This was the first time Jessica had talked with a cop. She'd never even been pulled over for a traffic ticket. She hadn't been questioned by Curry or anyone else after Holly's death because she hadn't been a close friend. She'd known, though, that a lot of the kids at school had been questioned, including Kent, Monica, and Carmen.

"Detective Curry," she said, "who was it in the ravine?"

He eyed her levelly. "Carmen Briggs."

Jessica gasped. "*Carmen?* Oh, my God."

"Let's sit down, Jessica," he said.

Detective Curry led Jessica into the living room and they sat on the couch.

"Was she mur—" She couldn't say the word.

"We don't know," Curry replied. "She was walking home from a pom-pom squad meeting at Tracy Willis's house that was over at nine-thirty. She apparently fell from the bridge over the ravine. It isn't clear whether she fell accidentally or was pushed off the edge. The autopsy may give us more information. But I think it's odd that she'd die just a month after her friend Holly Baldwin. Don't you?"

Jessica nodded, dazed.

"Are your parents here?" he asked.

"No," Jessica answered. "They're—they're out of town."

"Where?"

"Chicago. On a business trip."

"You alone?"

"For the rest of the week. They'll be back on Friday night."

"Jessica," he said, reaching into his suit and pulling out a small notebook, "Carmen's mother told me Carmen had been here just two nights ago. Very late."

Jessica nodded.

"Did she come here alone?"

"No. She came with Monica and Talley."

Curry scribbled in his notebook. "That would be Monica Sayles?"

"Yes."

"What's Talley's last name?" he asked.

"Johnson," Jessica said.

"Mmm hmm," he said, writing. Then he looked up from his pad. "What time did they come over?"

"I guess about eleven," Jessica said. "Maybe a little later."

"Why so late?"

"They—I mean, Monica wanted to—" She paused.

This was going to sound crazy. "Monica wanted us to use the Ouija board."

"Ouija board?" the detective said, cocking an eyebrow. "You mean, to contact spooks?"

"Yes."

"Any spook in particular?"

Jessica looked at the floor. "I know this sounds kind of silly, but Monica thought this spirit named Michael had spoken to her once before at her party."

"She used the Ouija board at a party?" he asked. "When was that?"

"Friday night," Jessica said. "And this spirit spoke—well, I mean, the planchette—do you know what I mean, the planchette?"

"I believe so, yes," the detective said. "That little contraption that slides around the board." He smiled. "I remember playing with a Ouija board when I was a kid."

Jessica nodded. "The planchette moved around and spelled out that Michael was there."

She watched the detective's face for a clue about what he was thinking, but Detective Curry would have made a good poker player. He wasn't giving anything away.

"Did this Michael have any words of wisdom at Monica's party?" asked Curry.

"He said that—that more will die."

"More?"

"Yes," Jessica said. "After Holly, I mean."

"Wasn't Monica Holly's best friend?" Curry asked.

"Yes, along with Carmen."

"Did you think it was a little bit strange that Monica would have a party so soon after Holly's death?"

"Well—" Jessica didn't quite know what to say. She didn't like Monica, didn't respect her, and was still very angry with her for accusing Kent of Holly's murder. But she didn't want to say anything that would incriminate her, either. Especially to someone who could have charges brought against her.

"Well," she said carefully, "I guess it *was* a little soon, but she—I guess she decided that life should go on. Holly was that kind of person, too. I'm sure that Monica felt terrible about Holly's death."

"Would you say that you're a good friend of Carmen's?" the detective asked.

"Not a close friend," Jessica said. "But I've known her since—well, forever. We've gone to school together since first grade."

"Did she have enemies that you know of?"

"Not that I know of," said Jessica. "I mean, she ran around with a group of kids who—who weren't always nice to everybody, but I sure don't know anyone who'd *kill* her."

"Did Carmen have any arguments with friends lately?" he asked.

Jessica hesitated. *Kent.*

"No." She'd said it too loud.

Detective Curry looked at her curiously. "You sure?"

The memory of Carmen's argument with Monica in the theater bathroom flitted through her mind.

"I'm sure," Jessica said.

Was she doing the right thing? She didn't want to implicate Monica and she certainly wasn't going to say anything that could hurt Kent.

"I talked with Monica late last night," Curry said. "She says she's getting threatening notes."

Jessica caught her breath. *Did Monica tell Curry she suspected Kent?*

"She thinks she knows who's been writing them," Curry said. Jessica was aware that he was watching her face closely. "I understand you're now going with Kent Andrews."

"Yes," Jessica said stiffly. Monica *had* implicated Kent!

Jessica realized she was beginning to tremble with anger. She had to get herself in control. Maybe Curry was pushing her to see how soon she'd break.

"You think Kent's responsible for those threatening notes?" Curry asked.

"*No!*" Jessica cried. "Absolutely not!" Suddenly, she didn't care about staying in control.

"Would he have any reason to dislike Carmen that you know of?"

"No!"

"Would *you* have any reason—?"

"No," Jessica said. *Was she a suspect?*

"Jessica, I'm talking to a lot of people about these deaths—Holly's and Carmen's. I'm asking a lot of the same questions. Where were you last night between nine-thirty and ten?"

Jessica stared at Detective Curry. "Here."

"Alone?"

"Yes, watching TV."

"I'm going to give you my phone number." Detective Curry reached into his pocket and handed her a business card. "Call me if you think of anything that might help us."

Jessica took the card.

"I'll be talking to you again," Curry said.

He stood and strode to the front door. He put a hand on the doorknob, paused, and turned to face Jessica.

"By the way," he said, "what did Michael have to say to you girls on Saturday night?"

Jessica felt the blood drain from her face. Feeling a little faint, she grabbed the edge of the couch and took a deep breath. "Monica asked if she would be the next person to die."

"And?"

"The Ouija board—Michael said—" She couldn't go on.

Detective Curry's voice was soft. "What did Michael say, Jessica?"

"Michael just said one word." Jessica felt her throat constrict and she coughed.

"Yes?"

Jessica cleared her throat. "He said, 'Carmen.'"

Detective Curry's face didn't change. "Smart spook," he said. Then he nodded to Jessica and disappeared out the front door.

CHAPTER 9

Everybody knew about Carmen's death when Jessica arrived at school. The kids were clustered in small groups around the student parking lot, the front steps, the flagpole, and down the halls of Greenwood High talking about it. Jessica heard the excited, frightened voices saying the key words as she hurried through the school looking for Kent: *Carmen, murdered, ravine, TV, Holly, killer . . .*

Jessica had tried to call Kent after Detective Curry had left her house, but Mrs. Andrews said that Kent had already left for school. It was time, she knew, to stop waiting and hoping for everything to resolve by itself. It was time for action, time to talk to Kent, to demand some answers. She couldn't help him if she didn't know what was going on.

Jessica searched the halls near his locker, his first-period classroom, and the gym trying to find him. Finally, she spotted him and Tom in a close huddle in front of the Media Center on the second floor.

"Kent!" Jessica cried. "I've been looking for you!"

Kent and Tom immediately stopped talking and whirled around to face her, and a small blue notebook fell from Tom's hands to the floor. He dove down to scoop it up.

"Here," he said to Kent. He opened the little book, tore out the first two pages, then thrust the book at Kent. "I'll—put these away." He folded the pages once and tucked them into his heavy world-history text book.

"Hi, Jess," Kent said, pocketing the miniature spiral. He stood awkwardly, his face flushed, and folded his arms over his chest.

"Hi, Jess," said Tom.

"Hi," Jessica said. She looked at Kent, then Tom. What was so important about that notebook?

Then it hit her. Holly's "magic notebook"! Is that what the guys had?

Jessica suddenly felt a little light-headed.

"What's up?" Kent asked.

"Uh . . ." She rubbed her forehead. *Get hold of yourself!* she thought. Then she remembered why she'd looked for Kent, why she had to talk to him. "Did you hear about Carmen?" she managed to say.

"Yeah," Kent answered. "It's terrible."

"Detective Curry came by my house early this morning," Jessica said.

Kent's eyes widened. "*Your* house? Why did he want to talk to *you?*"

"Because," Jessica said, her mind now focused on what she was saying, "Carmen's mother told him she'd been over at my house late on Saturday night."

Kent frowned. "Saturday night?" he said. "After the movie?"

"Yes," Jessica said. "She came with Monica and Talley. Monica wanted all of us to use the Ouija board again."

Kent looked completely disgusted. "That figures."

70

"But Kent," Jessica said urgently, "Detective Curry mentioned *you*."

Kent blinked. "What'd he say?"

"He was asking about you and Holly."

"Yeah?"

"Monica told him about the threatening notes she's been getting," Jessica said.

"Did she tell him that *I* sent them?" Kent asked.

Jessica nodded. "I think so."

"What did *you* tell him?"

"Nothing," Jessica said. "How could I? Kent, I don't know what's going on!"

Kent shook his head and stared at the floor. "I'm sorry, Jess."

"Kent," Jessica said, "Curry is questioning everybody. He even asked *me* what I was doing last night between nine-thirty and ten."

Kent looked up at her. *"You?"* He was obviously upset. "Why you?"

Jessica leveled her gaze at him. "You'd better be ready to tell him what you were doing, too."

"I was at Tom's house," Kent said quickly. Tom's mouth opened and he turned to look sharply at Kent. But he didn't say anything. "Right?" Kent looked hard at Tom.

Tom stared back at Kent and then nodded. "Yeah," he said. "We were together. At my house."

Jessica's heart began thundering in her chest. Kent and Tom were acting so guilty. But they were innocent! *Weren't they?*

"Kent, I have to ask you something." Jessica took a deep breath. "And I want you to be very honest with me."

"Okay," Kent said. He eyed her keenly.

"What was Holly's 'magic notebook'?"

Tom glanced at Kent, his eyes fearful.

"Who told you about that?" Kent asked.

"I heard some kids talking," Jessica said evasively. "What's it all about?"

"The kids are talking about it?" He seemed surprised. And alarmed. Kent took a deep breath and blew it out. He glanced at Tom and then back at Jessica. "Holly worked in the school office last summer—"

"Kent!" Tom said sharply.

"It's okay," Kent said to Tom. "This is *Jessica.*"

"You're not going to tell her!" Tom insisted.

"Just a minute," Kent said to Jessica. He nudged Tom and they walked partway down the hall. They talked softly, urgently, obviously arguing.

Voices in Jessica's mind were whispering at her, but she didn't want to listen. *Kent is innocent! Kent didn't do anything wrong!* she kept saying to herself, trying to drown out the voices that were murmuring warnings at her. *I've known him since first grade!*

Kent and Tom apparently settled their argument. Tom stayed where he was, his hands on his hips, and Kent returned to Jessica.

Please, Kent, Jessica pleaded to him silently, *please tell me something I can believe!*

"Jessica," Kent said, lowering his voice, "I'm going to tell you everything, but I just can't do it now."

Jessica's heart sank. "Why not?"

"I—I could get some good people in a lot of trouble."

"Are you talking about *yourself,* Kent?" Jessica said, feeling a wave of anger and frustration wash over her.

"I can't say." He put a hand on her arm, but she shook it off. "Jessica, I care about you very much. You know that, don't you?"

"No," said Jessica. "I used to think so, but I don't know that anymore. You've been acting so strange lately, and you won't tell me anything!"

"Do you trust me, Jessica?"

"How *can* I?" Jessica cried. "How can I trust you? Monica tells me you're sending her threatening notes, she's convinced you killed Holly, Detective Curry shows up at my house to talk about you, you're so distracted you can hardly communicate anymore, and when I ask you what's going on, you say you can't tell me!" She glared furiously at him. "What am I *supposed* to think about you?"

Kent's face had turned redder and redder as Jessica spoke.

"Fine, great," he said. "You think whatever you want to think. But I'll tell you something that's the honest truth. You're the nicest girl I've ever known. I love you, Jess. I should've said it before any of this happened so you'd know I mean it."

Jessica's heart could have stopped at that moment. She took a step back and stared at Kent. He had never said *I love you* before. She wanted so badly to believe him, to believe that he was in love with her. She'd dreamed for years of hearing him say those words to her.

But now she wasn't sure she believed him. Was he just trying to mollify her? To keep her on his side? To keep her from talking to the police?

She didn't trust herself at that moment. She didn't know what she wanted: to cry, to scream, to run away, to throw herself into Kent's arms. So she did none of those things.

She backed up a few steps without saying a word. Then she turned and walked away very quickly down the hall toward her locker.

The first bell rang then and she stopped in front

of her locker, her mind still dazed. She whirled the lock, unable to remember her combination.

She played the scene with Kent over in her mind. He loved her. Or did he? If he was innocent, why was he acting so guilty?

She remembered her combination then and opened her locker. Her first class was world history, so she pulled down the big history text and her notebook and headed for class.

She took her seat at the back of the classroom and waited. She didn't want to talk to anyone, not even Talley right now. She knew she wouldn't be able to hold a conversation and she felt disoriented because part of her mind was still on the second floor with Kent.

The classroom began to fill up quickly. Tom came in and smiled at Jessica as if nothing had just happened. He flopped into his seat across the aisle from her. Jessica glanced over at him and saw the pages he'd torn from the mysterious little notebook. They were still sticking out the top of his history book.

If only she could get hold of those pages! If they were from Holly's "magic notebook," they just might give her the clues she needed to fit all the jumbled pieces of the puzzle together.

Ted Thorson had just walked into the classroom. He was always a little late because he spent a half hour before school working in the Media Center. He was talking with Josh Tristan.

An idea sprang into Jessica's mind. It might work, but she'd have to act quickly. Class was about ready to start. She opened her purse and fished out her assignment notebook. It was the same size as the pages in Tom's textbook. She tore out two pages and folded them. If she could just pull a fast switch—

She got up and hurried to Ted, who was still standing in the front of the room. Josh had left him to go sit down.

"Ted, please do me a favor," Jessica whispered. "It's important."

"Sure, Jess," he said.

"Distract Tom for a minute. I'm going to do something, and I'll explain it all later, okay?"

Ted grinned. "A practical joke, right?"

"Well, not exactly, but—will you do it?"

"When?" he asked.

"Right now?"

Ted shrugged. "Sure, okay."

Ted walked to the back of the classroom and sat down in his seat next to Tom. Jessica watched him discreetly untie his shoelace. Then he stood up and took a few steps toward the front of the room and "tripped" over his shoelace, making a big production with his pratfall. He yelled, and, arms flailing, grabbed for the desks on either side of him, bringing one of them down on top of himself.

A couple of girls shrieked, and the attention of everyone in the room, including Tom, was immediately on Ted. Several girls rushed to his side, asking him if he were all right.

That was Jessica's cue. She moved quickly down the aisle with the pages torn from her notebook in her hand. With Tom's attention on the other side of him, she walked up to Tom and stopped at his side. She reached out her hand to pull out the notebook pages in his textbook.

"Okay, everybody," Mrs. Williams said from the front of the class. "Ted's okay, so let's get started."

Tom turned to look at the teacher, and Jessica snatched her hand back.

Without the pages. She'd blown it!

Everyone took their seats and Ted glanced at Jessica with a grin as if to say, *How'd I do?*

Jessica smiled a little, but shook her head. He frowned.

What was she going to do now? Ted had given her the perfect opportunity to switch the pages in Tom's textbook, but she hadn't been fast enough.

She *had* to get those pages from Tom!

The class period dragged on endlessly, and she didn't hear a word Mrs. Williams said. Every few minutes, she stole glances at Tom's book to see whether the pages were still there. He didn't touch them.

She wouldn't get another chance, she thought glumly. The next period was American lit, and Tom wasn't in her class then or in any other class until the afternoon. By that time, he would've taken his history book back to his locker and exchanged it for the texts in his afternoon classes.

A feeling of great sadness enveloped her. She was so confused about her feelings for Kent, and so in the dark about what was going on. She felt very much alone.

The bell finally rang, ending the class. She gathered up her books, vaguely aware that Ted had hurried on past her up the aisle. She heard some laughter at the front of the room and heard someone say, "Thorson, are you really running for class president?"

Jessica looked up. Ted had just written TED THORSON FOR SENIOR CLASS PRESIDENT on the blackboard.

"That's me!" he called out, waving at everybody. "I'm running for president, and you couldn't vote for a better candidate." He glanced at Jessica and nodded very slightly to her.

He's giving me a second chance! Jessica realized.

She looked over at Tom who still sat in his seat, watching Ted with a big grin on his face.

"Vote for me!" Ted called out. "You won't be sorry!"

Tom stood next to his desk, applauding. "You've got my vote, Thorson!" he yelled. "Unless someone better-looking runs!"

Jessica, her heart pounding, stepped up to Tom's side. With a quick movement, she snatched the notebook pages from Tom's book and replaced them with the pages from her own notebook.

She did it! She had the "magic notebook" pages!

She quickly tucked the mystery pages into her purse and hurried up to the front of the class, where kids were filing past Ted.

"You just name it," she whispered to Ted. "Anything I can do for you—you name it, and I'll do it."

"Great," he mumbled out the side of his mouth. "Because you owe me big, Reynolds. Now I have to run for class president! I *hate* student government!"

CHAPTER 10

Jessica hurried to her American literature class and took her seat in the back corner. Only a few other students had arrived, so she felt secure about getting out the notebook pages. She pulled them from her purse, unfolded them, and began to read.

She blinked.

They didn't make sense.

She reread them. The two pages were written in Holly's handwriting and appeared to be instructions for getting into a computer program.

Jessica knew a little about computers, so she recognized what the words signified. But she didn't know what kind of program this was.

Jessica stared out the window. *Holly was involved in something*, Monica had said. A computer program? Kent had said she'd worked in the school office over the summer, so the program probably was in the school's computer.

What would interest Holly in Greenwood High's computer programs?

Jessica sat up as the realization struck her.

Greenwood High's grades! They were all on computer. *She must have been tampering with the grades*.

That would make sense. All Holly talked about was getting into an Ivy League school and going to law school. She could make sure she'd be able to do that with straight A's.

But didn't she have nearly straight A's already? Jessica thought about it. No, she had received a B-plus in sophomore chemistry. And there had been a B in—what was it?—freshman English. Jessica remembered because Holly had loudly complained that her teachers had been grossly unfair, had not liked her and given her lower grades out of spite.

Jessica wondered if those grades were now listed as A's.

There was one way to find out. She would have to talk with Ted Thorson again. He worked with the computer system all the time in the Media Center. He could easily plug into the student-grade program if he had these instructions and access code.

Talley walked into the classroom then and took her seat next to Jessica.

"You heard about Carmen?" Talley said.

Jessica nodded. "Yeah."

"I can't believe what's happening around here!" Talley looked at Jessica with concern in her eyes. "How're you doing?"

"Okay," Jessica said, shrugging.

Monica entered the classroom then, spotted Jessica, and hurried over to her.

"Detective Curry talked to you this morning?" she whispered anxiously.

Good news travels fast, Jessica thought.

"Yeah," she answered.

"And he asked you about Kent?" Monica was staring intently at Jessica.

"Who told you?" Jessica asked.

"Tom. Curry asked you about Kent?"

"Yeah," Jessica said.

"Did he—did Curry mention me?" she asked.

"He wanted to know why Carmen was over at my house so late on Saturday night."

"Did you tell him I was there with her?"

"Yes," Jessica replied. "I told him about the Ouija board."

"Did you tell Curry what the Ouija board said?" Monica asked. "About Carmen?"

"He asked me," Jessica said, "so I told him." She thought Monica was pressing awfully hard for information.

Monica took a deep breath and blew it out. Jessica noticed that her hands shook a little. Was she afraid of what the police might find out?

"You worried?" Jessica asked, watching her face closely.

"The cops are talking about me—of *course* I'm worried!" she snapped.

"Detective Curry asked me where I was between nine-thirty and ten," Jessica said. "He'll ask you, too."

Monica's eyes opened wide. "I was—I was at a movie!" she said. "The Cinema Four had that new romantic film with—what's-her-name, the actress with all the dark hair."

"Who were you with?" Jessica asked.

"By myself!" Monica said, her voice rising in alarm. "Carmen had to go to a pom-pom meeting. You have any problem with that, Jessica?"

"I don't," Jessica said calmly. "The police might, though. They'll probably ask you if anyone saw you there."

Monica's face turned red, her expression one of great anxiety. "Alisa Anderson!" she cried. "She saw me there! She works at the concession stand."

80

That would be easy enough to check.

Jessica thought back to the argument she'd over-heard between Monica and Carmen in the movie theater's rest room. Carmen had told Monica she wasn't going to lie anymore, that she was going to tell the cops about Monica's fight with Holly just before Holly was murdered.

Could Monica have killed Carmen to keep her silent? And what had Monica and Holly fought about, anyway? Holly's tampering of the grades? Was Monica involved in that, too?

Their American lit teacher arrived then, and Monica took her seat across the room. Jessica glanced at Talley, who'd been listening to the conversation from across the aisle. Talley raised her eyebrows, obviously surprised at Monica's behavior.

Jessica leaned over to Talley and whispered, "I'm going to find out what happened. To Carmen *and* Holly."

Talley's eyes got big. "How?"

Jessica patted her purse. "I've got some information. I'll tell you about it later."

Jessica sat through class and thought about Kent, Tom, Holly, Carmen, and Monica—the kids she'd grown up with. It was hard to believe that two of them were dead. And even harder to believe that maybe one of them was probably a killer.

She couldn't—wouldn't—accept that Kent was guilty. Yes, he was acting strange, but she couldn't imagine that he was capable of gunning down a classmate in cold blood. For *any* reason.

Monica, though, was a different story. She was selfish and high-strung. If the circumstances were right, she just might be able to kill. She had no loyalty and was devoted to only one person: herself.

Jessica turned over the facts in her mind. Monica

had had a bad fight with Holly just before her death. She'd even slapped her. It was an argument that was bad enough that she didn't want the police to find out about it. Monica had accused Kent of the murder when she was questioned by Detective Curry. She claimed to have received threatening notes. But she could have sent them to *herself* so she could blame Kent.

And why did she appear at Jessica's late on Saturday night to consult the Ouija board? She claimed it was because she was scared about the threatening notes. But what if it was really because she wanted the Ouija board to tell everyone—who could act as witnesses—that Carmen was supposed to be the next victim?

Did she push the planchette to spell out the next victim, all the while knowing that she herself would do the killing?

Unless Carmen had just accidentally fallen from the bridge—and that was too much of a coincidence to believe—she was either murdered in a random killing or by someone who knew her.

Jessica was determined to check out Monica's story. It was the only way she could help Kent. She had to find out who killed Carmen and Holly.

"Hi, Alisa," Jessica said, sliding her money under the ticket window. "One, please. Theater Four." She grinned. "I love romances."

Alisa Anderson smiled shyly and took Jessica's money. "Hi, Jessica," she said. "I haven't seen it, but I hear it's a good movie."

Jessica had always liked Alisa but didn't know her well. Alisa was a little hard to get to know. She was very shy and unless you asked her lots of questions, there were long, uncomfortable pauses in the conversation. Jessica guessed Alisa didn't have a lot of self-confidence.

"Yeah," Jessica said, "Monica said she saw the nine-o'clock show last night." She paused. "Were you working then?"

"Uh huh," Alisa said. "Over in concessions."

Jessica didn't know how else to ask Alisa without simply being direct. "Did you see Monica?"

"Yeah." Alisa smiled with pleasure. "She talked to me for a while before the movie. I didn't think she even knew who I was."

So Monica was here just as she had said. It was strange, though, for her to talk "for a while" with Alisa, who was a very nice girl but considered a "nobody" by Monica and her friends. Monica didn't usually talk to nobodies unless there was something in it for herself.

Was she setting up an alibi? The thought flashed through Jessica's mind as if it had been lit up in neon lights.

Alisa slid the ticket under the window.

"Thanks," Jessica said. "Uh, Alisa, were you in the lobby when the movie was over?"

"Sure," said Alisa. "I helped close."

"Did you by any chance see Monica after the movie?" Jessica asked, trying to sound casual, but knowing she appeared awfully nosy.

"Yeah, I waved to her," Alisa said. She frowned, obviously wondering what all the questions were about.

"Thanks, Alisa," Jessica said, and left hurriedly before Alisa could ask her why she wanted to know so much.

Jessica pulled open the heavy glass doors to the Multiplex theater and stepped into the lobby. She looked at her watch. The movie was to start at nine o'clock, just as it had last night. That was in about three minutes.

Jessica walked past the concession stand, down a corridor, and into Theater Four. She chose a seat near the back, about three rows from the end by the far wall. If Monica had wanted to keep a low profile inside the theater, she'd have probably picked a seat near this one.

Monday night, like Sunday, was not a big movie night. In fact, there were only about a dozen people in the theater. Nobody watched Jessica come in.

Probably no one would notice her leaving.

Carmen had left the pom-pom meeting at nine-thirty, Jessica remembered Detective Curry saying. Carmen had started walking home from Tracy Willis's house about four blocks from the ravine in the park. It would've taken her roughly ten minutes to get to the footbridge. She was killed between nine-thirty and ten.

Could Monica have sneaked out of the theater after setting up an alibi with Alisa Anderson? Did she have time to drive to the footbridge, kill Carmen, and then hurry back to the theater before the movie was over?

That's what Jessica had come to find out.

The lights in the theater dimmed and the movie started. Jessica didn't get involved in the story, though. She wasn't there long enough for that.

After about ten minutes, Jessica got up quietly and moved out of the dark theater. The cinema building held four separate screens. The entrance to Theater Four was in the middle of a long corridor, out of sight from the lobby. The corridor was empty.

If Monica had sneaked out of the theater, most likely no one saw her leave.

Jessica reached into her purse and grabbed the

small piece of thin cardboard and masking tape she'd placed there before leaving home. She hurried to the side exit door and slipped outside. She quickly taped the cardboard over the spring bolt in the door so that it wouldn't lock behind her, but it would shut completely. Then she ran to her car.

The park was probably a fifteen-minute drive away, so Monica would've had to take her car.

Jessica started up her old Dodge after some coaxing and drove to the park. She left her car in the dimly lit parking lot about fifty yards from the bridge over the ravine. She walked along the sidewalk to the ravine, the soft padding of her Adidas on the cement and the skittering of leaves over the grass the only noises in the night.

The footbridge was lighted with electric lanterns along the safety rail about every thirty feet. Jessica looked around her. Nobody was here. Most people in Greenwood were at home now watching TV with their families while kids worked on their schoolwork. Most would be in bed within the hour. It was that kind of town.

Jessica walked out over the bridge and looked down into the gloom. The ravine was filled with large oaks and scrub pines that towered over her and cast deep shadows below. The lighted footpath at the bottom of the ravine snaked its way through the darkness like a reptile glowing from within with a mercury-vapor brightness. Everything on either side of the path was hidden in deep shadows.

Carmen had fallen from here. She would have plunged to the bottom and broken her neck on the footpath below. Jessica shivered. It was an eerie feeling, standing there in the spot where she'd fallen from—or was pushed from. *The scene of the murder*. Jessica didn't want to stand here any longer.

A twig snapped behind her and Jessica whirled around. The sound had come from a clump of bushes at the edge of the ravine not far from the sidewalk.

Jessica's heart began beating fiercely in her chest. *Was someone standing behind the bushes watching her?*

CHAPTER 11

"Hello?" she called out.

No answer.

"Is anyone there?"

Silence.

If she walked back the way she came, she'd have to pass within ten feet of the bushes where she'd heard the noise. The only other escape was to cross to the opposite side of the ravine, away from her car.

She stood frozen for half a minute wondering what to do. She could have imagined the noise, she told herself. But she didn't think so. She was definitely jumpy, but her mind wasn't likely to have invented a noise that wasn't there.

It could have been only a rabbit or squirrel in the brush. Or maybe the wind rustling some leaves.

But what if it *was* someone standing behind the bushes? What if a killer—the same person who murdered Holly and Carmen—was hiding in the bushes, ready to claim another victim?

Jessica knew she had to get to her car. Should she run toward her car and hope the person behind the bushes wouldn't chase her? She was wearing jeans and running shoes, and had competed well in track last spring, so there was at least a chance she'd be able to get to her car safely.

And maybe the person behind the bushes was harmless. Maybe it was a homeless person who didn't want to get caught loitering in the park at this hour.

She listened for any slight noise, a foot shifting on the ground or heavy breathing. But all she could hear was the hammering of her own heart.

She reached into her purse and grasped her car keys. She'd read that, placed between the fingers in a clenched fist, keys could act like brass knuckles in defending oneself. She tucked her purse under her other arm and readied herself to run.

She took a deep breath and let it out.

Then she started off, running as fast as she could to the end of the bridge nearest the bushes, past them, and down the sidewalk to the parking lot. She couldn't hear running steps behind her, but she didn't dare look over her shoulder to see if she was being chased. It could cost her a second or two—and her life.

She reached the car—she hadn't locked it—scrambled inside, and locked the doors.

Only then did she give herself the chance to look toward the ravine. She saw no one.

The sidewalk was empty.

She was breathing heavily and drenched in sweat, not from the effort of running, but from sheer terror. She jammed the key into the ignition and turned it.

Thankfully, the engine roared to life on the first try. She peeled out of the parking lot and headed for the theater complex.

Her breathing began to slow when she was about halfway back.

That was ridiculous, she scolded herself. *There was nobody there. I probably just imagined it.*

It must have been a rabbit in the bushes, even more afraid than she was.

She drove back to the theater and parked near the side exit. She found the spring bolt still taped with the cardboard in place. She ripped off the cardboard and let herself back inside the theater corridor. It was empty, just as she had hoped, and she made her way to Theater Four and slipped inside.

The movie was still on. She found her seat and sat down. She checked her watch. It was 10:03.

She'd done it. She'd demonstrated how Monica Sayles could have killed Carmen Briggs last night and gotten back to the theater with time to spare.

Jessica sat through the rest of the movie. She had missed so much of the story that she didn't understand what was going on. But that didn't matter. She was thinking about Monica, anyway. She was beginning to think of Monica as a murderer.

The movie ended at 11:05, and Jessica left with the other people in Theater Four. She waved good-bye to Alisa, just as Monica had the night before, and walked out to the parking lot.

Her car started on the second try, and she headed home. Kent's house was on her route, and she slowed a little as she passed. His car wasn't parked in the front the way it usually was. He must have been out. Jessica wondered where he was.

She drove home and pulled into the garage. She got out of the car and heard Ish through the kitchen door. The dog wasn't barking joyfully the way she ordinarily did.

She was crying instead.

"Ish!" Jessica called out, alarmed.

She unlocked the door and pushed it open. Ish

stood in the kitchen, her face bloodied, and her right eye half-shut. Her tail swung slowly back and forth in spite of her wounds.

"Ish! My God, what happened to you?" Jessica cried. She scooped up the dog in her arms and carried her into the kitchen. She put the dog on the counter next to the sink and examined her face. The wounds didn't appear deep. Ish whimpered and stared with trustful eyes at Jessica, then licked her hand and continued to swing her tail.

"Thank God you're all right, Ish. We'll go see Dr. Schmitt first thing in the morning before school. I'll call his answering service tonight."

She picked up the dog again and turned toward the dining room. From where she stood, she could see the drapes in the dining room fluttering in the breeze.

The window.

She hurried into the dining room with Ish, and, feeling a crunching under her feet, pulled back the drape.

The window was broken. Jagged shards of glass framed a large hole in the window, littered the carpet, and glittered in the dim light cast from the kitchen.

Someone had broken in. *Was the intruder still in the house?*

Jessica, still holding Ish, took a few tentative steps toward the living room. Everything looked as it should. Nothing out of order, nothing missing that Jessica could see. She slid open a drawer in the buffet along the far wall. All of her mother's good silver was there, neatly stored the way it should be. She slipped a carving knife out of the next drawer.

Ish whimpered and Jessica hugged her tighter. The

dog wriggled to get free. Jessica walked back to the kitchen and put her down.

"Stay in here while I check the house," she said, then closed the swinging door to the dining room.

She moved back through the dining room, clutching the knife tightly, and then tiptoed into the living room, turning on lights as she walked. The television was there, and so was the stereo with its CD and tape player.

"It wasn't a thief," Jessica murmured.

She moved into the foyer and saw the front door. It stood ajar. She hurried to it and peeked outside. She saw no one on the front porch, no one in the yard. She closed the door and bolted it.

Whoever broke in, left by the front door. She was relieved to realize she was alone in the house. At least, she hoped so.

The sun room, just off the foyer, was empty, as was the rest of the main floor. Nothing taken; nothing out of place.

Jessica stood at the bottom of the stairs and looked up into the darkness at the top. She flipped on the upstairs hall light from the bottom of the steps, then slowly started up the flight of stairs.

It didn't make sense that someone would break into the house, hurt Ish, and leave without taking anything.

Or didn't they have time? Maybe the intruder heard her drive up and ran out of the house.

She reached the top step and looked around. The doors to each of the three bedrooms stood open. From where she stood she could see into her parents' room. It looked untouched. So did the guest room.

She slowly started down the hall to her room, and her heart began hammering louder and harder.

The first thing she saw was a teddy bear from her

91

stuffed animal collection, lying in the doorway, face-down. She moved closer. A poster that had been hanging on her wall was torn into small pieces and scattered next to the bear.

Jessica reached the doorway to her room and froze.

The room had been ransacked. Her bed had been stripped, the sheets torn from the bed and thrown on the floor. The books from the shelf over her desk had been thrown into every corner. The globe on her desk was smashed on the floor next to her bed. Even the clothes from her closet had been tossed in every direction, some of them ripped to shreds.

"Why?" Jessica whispered, a lump forming in her throat. *"Why?"*

A piece of paper, torn from a spiral notebook, caught her eye on top of her bed. Numbly, she walked closer. There were words scrawled on the paper in black Magic Marker.

MIND YOUR OWN BUSINESS! it said. OR YOU WILL BE NEXT!

CHAPTER 12

"I know it's late," Jessica said. "Thanks for coming over."

"Wow," Talley said, standing in the doorway to Jessica's room, surveying the damage. "Are you going to call the police?"

"You're not going to believe this," said Jessica, "but, no."

Talley turned to stare at Jessica. "Why not? Aren't you scared?"

"Yes, I'm scared," Jessica replied. "But not for the reason you're thinking."

"What do you mean?"

Jessica stepped over a pile of cassettes with their tapes pulled out and trailing over the floor. She walked to her bed and slid her hand under the mattress. She drew out the two small sheets of notebook paper and held them up.

"This is what he—or she—was looking for," she said.

"What is it?" Talley joined Jessica in the middle of the room.

"The instructions and access code for getting into Greenwood High's computer system," Jessica said.

"I think Holly got hold of this somehow and was monkeying with her grades."

"Wow," Talley said again. "And you think that's why your room was tossed?"

Jessica nodded. "Yeah. And Ish was hurt. I can't think of any other reason."

"Is Ish going to be all right?" asked Talley.

"I think so," Jessica answered. "The wound on her head looks superficial, and her eye is open wider than when I got home. But I'll take her to Dr. Schmitt tomorrow before school."

"Who knew you had these computer instructions?" Talley asked.

"I swiped them from Tom," Jessica said. "I think he probably figured out who took them."

"Do you think *Tom* could have done this to your room?" Talley said.

Jessica looked around. "I don't know."

"How did he get the instructions?"

"I don't know that either, for sure," Jessica said. "I think from Holly." She paused a moment, debating whether she should say any more. "You see," she said slowly, "I saw Tom and Kent with these pages earlier this morning."

"Kent?" Talley said. "Do you think he was changing his grades, too?"

Jessica sighed deeply. "I don't know."

"Do you think this has something to do with Holly's death?" Talley asked.

Tears filled Jessica's eyes. "I just don't know," she said. "I can't believe Kent could've gotten involved in murder, but he's been acting so—weird lately. He won't talk to me, won't tell me anything."

Talley hugged Jessica. "I'm sorry," she said. "Kent seemed like such a nice guy."

94

Jessica pulled away. "He *is* a nice guy!" she said, wiping her wet cheek with the back of her hand. "But I can't go to the police about this break-in, don't you see? Curry would ask me lots of questions I wouldn't want to answer."

"Yes, I see." Talley jerked her chin toward the intruder's note that was still on the bed. "Kent—whoever broke in here—says to mind your own business or you'll be next."

"That's just a threat," Jessica said.

"Don't you think he means it?"

"I don't know who wrote it!" Jessica exclaimed. "But if Kent *did* write it, he wrote it to protect me."

"He broke in here, tore up your stuff, and left a threatening note to *protect* you?" Talley said. "Jessica, you're not thinking straight."

"Maybe it was the only way he could warn me," Jessica said defensively. She knew, though, how stupid she sounded. She knew that Kent was involved in this thing. She didn't know exactly how or what he was guilty of, but she was ready to admit now that he was not the blameless innocent she'd *wanted* to believe he was.

"I'm not giving up," Jessica said stubbornly.

"You're not giving up on Kent?" Talley said.

"I'm not giving up on finding out the truth," Jessica replied. She blew her nose and leveled her gaze at Talley. "I'm more determined than ever to get to the bottom of this. If Kent is a murderer, I want to know. If Monica is a killer, I want to know. If they're working together, if Tom is involved, if something else is going on that I don't know yet, I want to know. *I want to know what's going on!*"

* * *

"Do these instructions mean anything to you, Ted?" Jessica said.

She stood next to Ted Thorson, who was working in the school's Media Center office. The room was small and cramped and crowded with stacks of books, catalogs, and file folders. Ted looked up from his computer monitor and read the pages Jessica had handed him.

"These instructions get into Greenwood's computer files," he said.

"Any particular files?" Jessica asked.

"Not any that *I* work on," Ted said. "Let's see." He smiled. "This is a clever access code. It changes every day." He pointed to the instructions. "See? You add the numbers in the date and then type in the class code. You want the senior class?"

"Yes," said Jessica.

He entered the numbers and stared at the monitor.

"My God, where did you get these instructions?" he said.

"They get into the grade records, don't they?" Jessica said.

"They sure do."

"That's what I thought." She walked around the small table where Ted sat so she could face him.

"Ted, will you promise me something?"

"Sure," Ted said, studying the monitor. "What?"

"I need to find out some things," Jessica said. "These instructions were Holly's, and I think she changed her grades last summer while she was working in the school office."

"Want me to check her records?" Ted asked.

"Yes," Jessica said. "But what we learn here is just between you and me. Okay?"

"Sure," said Ted.

He went back through the senior class and stopped on Holly Baldwin.

"What grades are we interested in?" he asked.

"Freshman and sophomore years," Jessica said.

He tapped the keyboard and Holly's freshman grades flew up on the monitor.

"All A's," he said.

"She changed them," Jessica said. "She didn't get straight A's that year."

"Sophomore year's the same." Ted looked up at her. "Anybody else?"

"Monica Sayles," said Jessica. "She didn't earn straight A's either."

Ted typed in Monica's name and began scanning through her grades.

"All A's," he said, "in the sophomore class."

"Have you ever known Monica to be a 4.0 student?" Jessica said.

"No," Ted replied. "She's a pretty good student, but not *that* good. Here, in her junior year, there're some B's."

Jessica leaned in and studied the screen. "I wonder why these grades weren't changed?"

"Maybe Holly only *improved* other people's grades," Ted said, "while she *perfected* herself."

"How about Carmen?"

Ted glanced sharply at Jessica. "Are you thinking what I *think* you're thinking?"

"I don't know if there's a connection between this grade scam and the murders," Jessica said. "I just want to see what I can learn in these files."

Ted typed in Carmen's name, and her list of grades appeared on the monitor.

"Not changed," he said. "Lots of B's and C's here."

"Let's look at Tom Finch's grades," said Jessica.

She glanced at the clock. "We'd better hurry. First period starts soon. I meant to be here earlier, but I had to take my dog to the vet," she said, watching the screen. "And call the glass company. I have a broken window that needs fixing."

"Here he is," Ted said. "Geez, his grades are really bad."

Jessica studied the grades listed for Tom and frowned. "It doesn't make sense," she said, fascinated with the figures on the monitor. "Tom's not a great student, but these grades are barely passing!"

"Do you think Holly changed Tom's grades for the worse?" Ted asked. "You know, I hate to say it, but Holly really *could* be a bitch sometimes."

Blackmail. The word leaped out of a dark corner of Jessica's mind where it had been hiding for several days. Carmen had mentioned blackmail when she argued with Kent about Holly.

Did Holly make her friends pay her for good grades? Or did she threaten to change their grades if they didn't do what she wanted?

But that didn't make sense, Jessica thought. Occasionally, there were computer errors that marked incorrect grades on student records. It was easy to get those mistakes corrected by reporting it to the counselor's office.

Maybe Holly and Tom had had a fight, and she paid him back with the bad grades.

"Let's see Kent Andrews' grades," Jessica said.

Ted glanced up at her, obviously surprised. "Okay," he said. "You're the boss."

He tapped in Kent's name and scrolled down his list of grades.

Jessica, prepared for the worst, held her breath and concentrated on the monitor.

"Looks about right," Ted said.

He scrolled through sophomore year and junior year, and Jessica began to relax a little. When Ted was finished scanning the junior year, Jessica blew out the breath she'd been holding. *His grades hadn't been changed.*

But Tom's grades had certainly been changed.

"I don't understand what happened with Tom," Jessica said, half to herself.

"Tom's very familiar with computers," Ted commented. "I'm surprised he was involved with Holly on this. If he could get access to one of the school's computers, he could have gotten into the grade program by himself."

"That's it!" Jessica exclaimed.

"What?"

"He figured out *how* to get into the system," Jessica said. "But he needed Holly. She had access to the computers!"

"Right," Ted said, nodding. "That makes sense."

"Tom created a monster," Jessica went on. "After Holly learned the codes and changed her grades and his, maybe she started a little business—changing grades for a price."

"Tom wouldn't like that," Ted said. "He's a little goofy—I wouldn't be surprised if he changed *his* grades for the better—but he wouldn't charge other people to improve their grades."

"And he couldn't turn Holly in," Jessica said, "because *he* was the person who figured out the code! Holly did have *that* on him." She paused. "I'll bet he was furious with Holly. He already disliked her—and Carmen and Monica—because they made fun of his height."

Ted sat thoughtfully a moment before he spoke. Finally, he asked what Jessica herself had been thinking. "Do you think Tom had something to do with Holly's murder? Or Carmen's?"

Jessica shook her head. "I can't believe that Tom's involved in murder," she replied. "But I just don't know, Ted. I just don't know."

CHAPTER 13

All during first period, Jessica thought about what she'd learned from the computer. Holly's grades were perfect; Monica's improved; Carmen's untouched; Kent's untouched; and Tom's were terrible.

What did that tell her? That some people were favored by Holly and others not. Maybe the favored paid Holly for their good grades; others refused. Or perhaps Holly manipulated the grades at her whim, according to who she was getting along with on a particular day. It probably made her feel very powerful. Holly would have liked that feeling.

By the end of the first hour, Jessica had decided to talk to Monica and tell her what she knew. Maybe Monica would inadvertently give her even a small piece of information—something that might make it all clearer.

She got her chance next period in American lit. The class had been assigned a research paper and was excused to the Media Center to work. Shortly after the class arrived there, Jessica saw Monica take the winding stairway to the second floor, and she followed close behind.

At the top of the stairs were study carrels and

small tables along the outer edges of a room with nearly a dozen long stacks of book shelves.

"Monica," said Jessica, catching up at the top of the stairs, "I want to talk to you."

Monica stopped, cocked her head to one side, and looked at Jessica curiously. She shifted her books and notebooks to the other arm. She must have sensed this was about something private because she said, "Okay. Where?"

Jessica beckoned her to follow and led her deep into the stacks at the far end of the room. Reaching the wall between the tall bookshelves, she turned around to face the other girl.

"I'll get right to the point," Jessica said. "I know all about Holly's 'magic notebook.' I know that Holly was changing grades for people."

Monica's expression didn't change, but Jessica saw her eyes widen with surprise—and something else. Was it fear?

"Okay," Monica said with exaggerated unconcern. She shrugged. "So?"

"So," Jessica said. "I know that *your* grades for freshman year improved a lot over the summer. But your sophomore grades stayed about the same."

"You've *seen* the grades?" Monica asked. Jessica nodded. Monica stared at her a moment. Then she said, "Did you see who else's grades were changed?"

"Holly's, of course. She became a straight-A student."

"What about Tom?" Monica said, staring hard at Jessica. "Did you see *his* grades?"

"Yes," Jessica answered. "Maybe you can explain that to me. They're terrible."

"Yes, they are," Monica said calmly. "And he was *furious*."

"*I* would have been royally P.O.'d," Jessica said.

"Oh, Tom was more than P.O.'d," said Monica. "And I think your knight on a white horse was worse. I think Holly *died* because of Tom's grades."

"That's interesting," Jessica said. "A few days ago you thought Holly died because of a jealous ex-boyfriend. Now you're accusing *both* Kent and Tom of killing Holly because she was tampering with the grades?"

"I don't know which one of them killed her," Monica snapped, her face suddenly becoming red with anger, "but I know that either Kent Andrews or Tom Finch was responsible!"

"How can you be so sure?"

"They're best friends!" Monica cried. "They take care of each other. And because I'm getting threatening notes!"

"What if I told you," Jessica said, "that I know about the fight you had with Holly just before she was killed? I believe you slapped her in the face." Jessica leaned against the bookshelf next to her and leveled her gaze at Monica. "I don't think the police know about that particular fight."

"Damn Carmen!" Monica said, barely containing her rage. *"She told you, didn't she?"*

"No," Jessica said, "she didn't. Not directly, anyway."

Monica, gritting her teeth, shoved her hand angrily into the bookshelf, pushing books out the opposite side. A surprised grunt came from the other side, and Tom's face appeared in the empty space where the books had sat.

"Tom!" Jessica gasped.

Tom's face was chalk-white. He turned and disappeared down through the stacks.

"What was *he* doing here?" Monica said, her eyes

103

wild with fear. "He heard us! He knows I *know!*"
She gazed with horror at Jessica. "And you, too!"

Neither Tom nor Kent was in any more classes
that day. They had cut out of school.

At the end of the day, standing at her locker, Jessica overheard a group of girls talking several yards
away.

"Did you hear the news at noon?" a blonde junior
was saying.

"What?"

"The autopsy report is back on Carmen," the girl
said. "She died by a blow to the head *before* she
fell from the bridge."

"God, it's true then. She was murdered just like
Holly."

Jessica felt her stomach heave and she turned and
walked quickly away. She didn't want to think about
it. It was too awful.

She hurried down the hall toward the front door.
She wanted to get out of here, away from the other
kids. Away from anything reminding her of murder
and death.

She turned the corner and found Monica standing
at her locker. Monica was staring at something in
her hand. Her face was ashen. She glanced over her
shoulder then, spotted Jessica, and beckoned to her
frantically.

"Jess!" she said. "Come here!"

"What's the matter?" Jessica said.

Monica thrust the picture she was holding into Jessica's hands and collapsed against her locker. "I'm
next, Jessica," she whimpered. "Oh, God, it didn't
take them long to decide."

"It didn't take who long to decide?"

"Tom and Kent. After Tom heard us talking."

Jessica looked at the picture. It was the same second-grade picture she had on her shelf at home. It had been folded to fit through the louvered slot in the locker. There was a big circle drawn with a red felt-tipped pen around Monica as a little girl. YOU'RE NEXT! read the big red letters.

"Monica, you've got to take this to the police," Jessica said firmly. She knew that going to the police might result in Kent's arrest. Or Tom's. But it was time to stop finding excuses for them and get to the truth.

Even if Monica *had* sent herself the threatening notes, she most certainly didn't deliver this picture to her locker. Jessica was sure of that by looking at Monica's face. Monica's eyes looked haunted and her face was ghostly white. Monica would've had to be the world's greatest actress to pull *that* off.

Jessica had seen Monica in play tryouts last year, and, despite her general theatricality, she was no actress. In fact, she was so bad when she read the big death scene, all the kids at the auditions burst out laughing. Monica had stalked out of the auditorium beet-red and fuming.

But this scene was definitely for real. "Monica, take this to the police," she repeated.

"I'm scared," Monica whispered.

"I know," Jessica said. "Come on. I'll drive you to the police station."

"No, that's okay," Monica said. "I'll go myself."

"You sure?"

"Yeah. I'll be okay."

"I wouldn't mind," Jessica said.

"No." Monica shook her head. "I'll go."

"Okay," Jessica said. "But call me at home when you get back, okay?"

"Okay." Monica stared at the floor, seemed to

pull herself together, gathered what she needed from her locker, and closed it.

The two girls walked out of the school together to the student parking lot.

"Call me," Jessica said just before Monica drove away. "I'll wait to hear from you."

Jessica drove home. The house was locked up and everything seemed to be in order. She let Ish outside for a while, then applied the salve to the dog's face that Dr. Schmitt had given her that morning before school.

The man from the glass company came around four to fix the broken window in the dining room. After he left, Jessica sat at her desk and tried to study. But the words in her lit book blurred on the page, and she couldn't keep her thoughts focused on anything but the faces of the kids in her class. She fingered a pencil sitting on her blotter and thought about going to school through the years with all of them: Brit, Holly, Monica, Carmen, Tom—and Kent. She felt as if she had known each of them well, even though they were not all close friends. After all, she had spent the last thirteen years with a lot of them.

She looked up at her shelf. Her second-grade picture wasn't there. Where was it? She thought a moment. When was the last time she'd seen it?

She couldn't remember. Did she put it away when she cleaned up her room last night after it had been torn apart? No, she didn't remember setting it back in its place.

She turned in her chair and glanced around the room. The picture wasn't anywhere—on the dresser, her nightstand, her desk, her armchair.

Was it taken by the person who broke into her house?

Was the picture taken from her shelf the same one that had been left in Monica's locker?

Jessica was startled by the phone ringing. She got up from her desk and hurried to her phone next to the bed.

"Hello?"

"Jessica!" It was Monica, whispering.

"Did you go to the police?" Jessica asked. "Did you show them your picture?"

"No," she said. "I didn't get there."

"Why not?"

"Because I know who killed Holly and Carmen!" Monica whispered.

Jessica sighed. "So what else is new?"

"What?"

"Monica," Jessica said impatiently, "you've told me twice already that you knew who committed the murders!"

"But now I'm almost sure!" she said. "Listen, this goes clear back to elementary school."

"What do you mean?" Jessica said.

"I have to be positive," said Monica. "I need to do something first. Can you be here at nine o'clock tonight?"

"Nine?" Jessica said. "Okay."

"Good," Monica said. "My parents will be out. It's their anniversary. They're going to the club for dinner and dancing."

"Are you going to tell them?" Jessica asked.

"As soon as I know for sure," Monica replied. "Just be here at nine."

"I'll be there," Jessica promised, and hung up. She collapsed on her bed. *What now?*

CHAPTER 14

Even though she wasn't hungry, Jessica fixed a light supper for herself. After eating, she sat with Ish in the living room and stared out the window into the trees.

She tried to keep her mind off of Tom and Kent, but her thoughts kept wandering back to the looks on their faces when she asked them about Holly's "magic notebook." They were definitely frightened that she knew something. *Holly's notebook had to be connected to the murders*.

Kent had obviously lied about where he was at the time of Carmen's murder. He'd said he was with Tom, but Tom had looked startled before hurriedly agreeing that they'd been together that night.

Could it have been Kent or Tom in the bushes at the ravine? Did one of them—or both—follow her from the movie theater to the park? She hadn't thought to check in the rearview mirror for a car that might have been tailing her.

Kent's car wasn't parked outside his house on her way home from the theater. *Maybe that was because he was at her house, tearing up her room*. Did he take the picture of their second-grade class so he could torment Monica with it?

Jessica decided she was ready for anything. Maybe Kent *was* a murderer. She would have to be ready to accept that if it were proven to be true. She'd resisted believing it could be possible for too long. Now it was time to let her head, and not her heart, take over for a while.

She flipped on the evening news and anchorwoman Bess Hartman announced Carmen's autopsy finding. The girls at school had heard it correctly; Carmen was killed by a blow to the head with a heavy, metallic object. Something like a tire iron, Hartman reported.

Jessica picked up the remote control on the coffee table and switched around from channel to channel, trying to find something to keep her mind off the murders. She settled on reruns of the "Bob Newhart Show." It was just what she needed.

She watched the clock all evening and wondered what Monica was doing. She'd said she needed to be positive about the identity of the person—or people—who murdered Holly and Carmen. Jessica couldn't believe that, after Monica's first two accusations, this one would be any more substantial. But she might as well hear what Monica had to say.

Finally, at 8:45 Jessica locked up the house, got into her car, and drove over to Monica's. The two-story Victorian house loomed up at the end of the driveway, silent and dark.

Jessica looked at her watch. Eight fifty-six, it said. Maybe Monica wasn't home yet.

Jessica parked the car at the front curb, shut off the motor, and waited. She rolled down the window and breathed the sweet autumn smells of the evening. *If only things were different,* she thought. If only Holly and Carmen were still alive and she was sitting with Kent, enjoying the evening and the closeness of him. The smell of his skin was a tangy mixture of masculine musky warmth and faint after-shave. She loved kissing him, running her fingers through his coarse, wavy hair.

That's enough! she thought. She shook her head to rid herself of the image of Kent's face and turned on the radio. She listened to music and watched the house. Five minutes went by.

Maybe Monica is at the back of the house and the light isn't showing from the street, Jessica thought. She got out of the car and walked up the front sidewalk. She rang the bell and waited. No one came. After ringing again and waiting a full minute, she started around the back of the house.

There was a light shining from the kitchen window at the back. Jessica moved up to the house, pushing through the evergreens under the window. She stood up on her toes and peeked inside. She could only see a small part of the kitchen. Nothing appeared to be out of order.

She walked to the back door and knocked. The door, which hadn't been shut all the way, swung open a few inches. Jessica's heart began hammering hard. Most people in this neighborhood not only closed their doors, but kept them locked up tight. Many even had alarm systems.

She gently pushed open the door and stepped inside. She was in the mudroom that led to the lighted kitchen.

"Monica?" she called.

There was no answer.

"Monica? It's Jessica."

No, God, don't let this be awful. Monica just can't hear me, right?

She moved up the four steps and into the kitchen. At first she saw nothing. The kitchen appeared to be empty. Until she moved around the island work area in the center of the room. Then she spotted the figure on the floor.

"Monica!" she gasped.

Monica was sprawled out on the vinyl floor, her face the color of old newspapers, in a widening pool of crimson liquid. In her hand was the picture from second grade that had been left in her locker that afternoon.

"Your parents home yet?" Detective Curry asked her, his hand placed gently on her shoulder.

Jessica, her eyes red from crying, sat on the couch in Monica's living room. She shook her head and fingered the wet wad of tissue in her hands. "Friday," she said, her breath coming out in ragged gasps. "Friday evening."

"I've got all the information I need from you right now," Curry said. "I want you to go home and call your parents. Tell them what's going on and have them come home now."

Jessica nodded. She didn't need to be told to summon her parents home. She was tired of trying to handle all of this by herself. It would be comforting to have her parents back home. She'd feel safer.

Jessica gazed numbly at Curry. "Do you think she'll live?"

"I don't know," Curry said. "The medics said she was in bad shape. I'm glad you got here when you did. If she does pull through, it'll be because of you."

Jessica stared at the floor. She didn't want compliments. She wanted Monica to survive.

"You make sure to lock all the doors and windows," Curry said. "And don't open the door to *anyone*." He paused and stared at her with serious intensity. "You don't know who to trust right now. I'll have a police officer escort you home."

He gestured to a young man in uniform. "Hagerty," he called out. "Would you follow this young woman home?"

The officer nodded.

"Thanks," Jessica said to Curry. She stood up and followed Officer Hagerty out the front door.

"It might take a minute to get my car started," she said to Hagerty. "It's been acting up a lot lately."

"No problem," he said.

He went to his patrol car, and she got into her car. It took four tries and some gentle encouragement, but the engine turned over. The officer followed her home, pulling up in the driveway behind her.

She called out the window to him, "Thank you."

He got out of his car, walked up to her open window, and leaned in. "Want me to check the house?"

Jessica was still trembling a little and was glad he offered. "Thanks," she said. "I'd really appreciate it."

She opened the garage door using the remote-control button in her car and drove in. Hagerty followed her inside the garage and she lowered the door behind them.

Ish barked her greeting as Jessica opened the door leading to the kitchen.

"Hi, girl," Jessica said. "This is Officer Hagerty."

The police officer scratched the dog behind the ears. "What kind of dog is this?" he said. "All-American?"

"Right." Jessica smiled. "That's a diplomatic description."

Jessica let Ish into the backyard and waited in the kitchen while the officer walked through the house, looking into closets and behind furniture, to determine that the house was okay.

"Thanks," Jessica said when he returned, "Ish probably would've let us know if something was wrong when we came in. But I appreciate your looking, anyway."

"Keep yourself locked in," the officer said.

"I will," Jessica promised. "Thanks." She let Ish back inside.

Officer Hagerty nodded and left.

Jessica moved directly to the phone in the living room and dialed the number of the Chicago hotel where her parents were staying.

"Yes, room number 408, please," she said to the hotel operator.

She waited and listened to the phone ring in their room. No one answered. She looked at her watch. It was nearly eleven. Maybe they'd gone to a show.

She decided to try again later.

She scooped up Ish in her arms and collapsed on the couch. "What a week," she murmured, scratching behind the dog's ears.

Ish looked up at her with big brown eyes and gave a low grunt of what Jessica took for agreement.

Jessica's thoughts turned to Monica. She must have been right about who the killer was. She must have checked out her theory and discovered the truth. The killer tried to murder her because of it.

It goes way back to elementary school, Monica had said on the phone. She had been clutching the second-grade picture while she lay on the floor. Was the killer in her second-grade class picture?

Ish, sitting next to Jessica, suddenly became alert, her body rigid.

"What is it?" Jessica said. She was aware that her own heart was suddenly thundering in her chest.

Ish bounded off the couch and ran to the door. There she froze, listening.

Jessica couldn't hear anything outside.

"What is it, Ish?" Jessica's voice cracked from nervousness.

Ish barked, then became quiet and cocked her head to listen again.

Jessica got up, moved to the front window, and drew the drape back to peer out. The lights were blazing behind her, so she couldn't see anything in the blackness beyond the window.

Ish began barking again, and this time she didn't stop. She barked and then paced closer to the door and barked louder.

"Someone's out there, I know," Jessica whispered. She backed away from the window and walked around the room, turning off the lights. Then, in the darkness, she moved back to the window and looked out.

Something was heaped on her front porch.

Ish had stopped barking now, but remained at her post by the front door.

"Someone left something on the porch," Jessica murmured. She walked to the front door and flipped on the porch light. Then she walked back to the front window and looked out.

She gasped.

A body was lying, apparently unconscious, on her front porch.

She hurried back to the door, unlocked it, and peered out.

She'd been wrong. It wasn't a person lying there. It was a dummy, *made up to look like herself*.

It was dressed in her clothes, clothes that had been taken from her room. A knife stuck out of the dum-

my's chest, and a red liquid—probably ketchup—
dripped off the dummy of Jessica and onto the porch.

And resting next to the dummy was a sign that
said, JESSICA, YOU'RE DEAD!

CHAPTER 15

Jessica shoved the door shut and locked it. She was trembling all over and her mind raced. *What should she do?*

She could call Detective Curry. But what would he say? Probably, *Just stay inside with the doors locked, and we'll investigate.*

But someone had gotten into her house before when the doors were locked. And by the time the police found out who the killer was, she could be dead!

She could call her parents to come home, but even if they left right now, they wouldn't get home till nearly dawn.

She had no intention of staying in the house tonight, trembling at every sound, waiting for someone to break in and kill her.

She had to get away from here. A safe place where no one would come looking for her, where she and Ish could wait until morning.

She had no close relatives in town, and Detective Curry was right about one thing: she didn't know who she could trust among her friends. If she found a family friend who would take her in, would she be

116

endangering another innocent person? She could never forgive herself if someone else was hurt.

No, it was better to find a safe place for herself and Ish. But where?

Turtle Lake. It was the perfect place! Her family's cabin was a ninety-minute drive from here. She could get there, lock herself inside, call her parents to come home, call the police about the dummy and the threat, and wait until morning.

"Come on, Ish," she said, running up the stairs. "We have a few things to pack."

Jessica, holding an overnight bag, opened the kitchen door leading to the garage.

"Come on, Ish," she said. Ish followed her happily through the door and into the garage. They got into the car, and Jessica locked all the doors.

Jessica turned the key in the ignition. The engine sputtered, then died.

"Come on, Baby," Jessica said, her voice trembling. "Let's go. When Mom and Dad get back, I'll take you into the shop. Just don't fail me now!"

She turned the key again and the car chugga-chugged and died.

"Come on, Baby, come on, Baby."

She turned the key and this time, with a little light pressure on the accelerator, the engine turned over and roared to life.

"Thank you," she said, sighing heavily. "Now let's get out of here."

She pushed the remote button and the garage door opened. She backed out slowly, looking around for any cars sitting at the side of the road or around near the front of the house.

The street was empty.

She drove down Fairview and onto Clairmont. It

wasn't until she'd driven three blocks on Clairmont that she even saw another car. It was parked in front of the 7-Eleven.

"Let's stop for some gas," Jessica said to Ish. "We're nearly empty."

She pulled into the 7-Eleven and parked next to the pump. She filled up her tank and paid for the gas inside. Then she got back into the car and, after two tries, got the car started.

She drove out into the street just as a familiar car pulled into the 7-Eleven lot.

Kent!

She lowered her head and kept driving. She didn't think he saw her, but she couldn't be sure. She pulled out into the light late-night traffic, and headed out of town.

She checked in the rearview mirror every couple of minutes, wondering if anyone was tailing her, but the road behind her was clear. Gradually she began to relax.

"I think we're okay now, girl," she said, stroking Ish, who had already fallen asleep in the passenger seat next to her.

It was a pretty ride up to the lake, even in the middle of the night. The full moon cast silvery shadows among the pine and birch trees that stood, like rows of towering soldiers, along the winding road. Once a deer leaped across the pavement in front of Jessica's car, but she was able to slow soon enough to avoid hitting it.

It took nearly an hour to get to Ryesdale, the closest town to the cabin. Jessica's stomach was rumbling painfully, reminding her that she'd eaten very little today. She also realized that she hadn't brought along any food for Ish.

Better stop at the Handimart, she thought. She

wouldn't need much, just a snack for tonight, something to eat in the morning, and a box of dog food.

It was nearly 1 A.M., and the place, ablaze with fluorescent lights, stood out starkly white against the blackness of its surroundings. Jessica parked next to the store and left her car running. She'd had so much trouble getting the car started to come up here, she didn't want to take the chance that it would finally refuse to move, stranding her in little Ryesdale without transportation and with only a twenty-dollar bill in her purse.

The store was empty except for the sleepy-looking young man working behind the counter. Jessica slid a package of doughnuts, a carton of orange juice, and a small box of dog food over the counter at him.

"You know the Whitmans?" Jessica asked, placing her twenty-dollar bill alongside her groceries.

"Sure," he said, ringing up her purchases.

Roger and Marge Whitman lived across the lake from her family's cabin. They lived there most of the year, except during January and February when they moved to their time-share condo in Florida.

"Are they home?" Jessica asked. "I mean, they're not traveling, are they?"

The young man shrugged. "Far as I know, they're home," he said. "They were just in yesterday."

"Good," Jessica said. The Whitmans were the closest people to her family's remote cabin, which was a little over twenty miles further down the road. Even though she was sure she hadn't been followed, she felt more secure knowing the couple was just across the lake from her.

Jessica got back into her car and pulled onto the main road again. Ish was sleeping peacefully, and Jessica felt safer than she had in the last few days.

She glanced in the rearview mirror. There was a

car behind her about a half mile away, but she wasn't worried. There had been light traffic on the road all the way up to the cabin. It was probably just a local driving home. She hoped the driver hadn't just staggered out of one of the bars that stayed open late along Main Street.

Twenty-three miles beyond Ryesdale, she turned into her lane. The dirt and gravel road was a mile long but seemed longer. It was narrow, only one lane, and was so bumpy and winding that it was necessary to slow to about twenty miles per hour. The headlights slashed through the night, throwing a brilliant beacon of light onto the road and the trees that crowded in on both sides. The car pitched gently from side to side, and Ish lifted her head to see what was going on.

"We're almost there," Jessica told her.

After a few more minutes, they rounded the last curve, and the family's cabin came into view. They called it "the cabin," but it was actually a lovely log home which nestled into a woody slope about thirty yards up from Turtle Lake.

Jessica parked in the drive behind the house, and she and Ish climbed out of the car. Jessica took in a deep breath of the air freshened with the moist scent of pine trees and lake water. Ish lifted her nose and wagged her tail and most of the rest of her, she was so excited. The dog loved the lake and was allowed to run loose on the paths down to the dock and over to the boat house.

"This time you'll have to stay with me," Jessica said. "Do what you have to do, and I'll wait. We've got to stick together."

Ish obediently found a good spot to relieve herself, then followed Jessica to the cabin door. Jessica unlocked the door, flipped on the light around the corner, and they went inside.

The living room was to the left of the door. It was carpeted, with family pictures and decorative lanterns on the log walls. The far left wall facing the lake was mostly glass from the floor to the ceiling, and undraped. It looked out to a narrow deck which ran along the cabin on three sides. In the far left corner was a raised stone fireplace.

Jessica set down her bag and locked the door behind her. She moved past the stairs leading to the loft where she'd slept as a child, and on to the kitchen area at the other side of the living room. She set the doughnuts and dog food on the counter and put the orange juice in the refrigerator.

"Make yourself at home, girl," Jessica said to Ish. "We'll be staying until tomorrow when Mom and Dad get back."

She went to the telephone on the wall next to the pantry to call her parents. It was going to worry them to get a phone call in the middle of the night, but it was necessary.

Just as she reached for the receiver, the phone rang shrilly, startling her. She snatched her hand back and stared at the phone. Who would call her at this hour? *Who knew she was here?*

Then she realized who it must be. The Whitmans. Maybe they were still up and saw her light from across the lake. She picked up the receiver.

"Hello?" she said.

No one spoke.

"Hello?" she repeated, her heart beginning to hammer hard.

There was a pause, then *click*. The caller hung up.

Jessica slowly hung up the phone, as heat and

adrenaline spread through her body. *Someone knows we're here,* she thought. *We're not safe now.*

She tried to think. Where could the call have come from? The nearest phones were in town, twenty-three miles away. Every bar had a phone, although she hadn't heard any loud background noises. The Handimart had a phone, and there was at least one phone booth on Main Street.

It *could* have been a wrong number. But wouldn't the caller have said something if that had been the case? Why did he wait for her to speak again before hanging up?

She must have been followed. The person who killed both Holly and Carmen, the person who tried to kill Monica, must have followed her to Turtle Lake. And now that person was on his way here to kill her, too.

She checked her watch. It was 1:40. It would take the caller at least twenty-five minutes, maybe thirty, to get to the cabin if he knew the way, Jessica thought.

Jessica realized that the cabin, isolated and standing between dense woods and Turtle Lake, was probably the most dangerous place for her to be, now that someone knew she was here.

We've got to go back home, she thought. She could drive directly to the police station and stay there until her parents returned.

"Come on, Ish," she said, hurrying across the living room to pick up her bag. "We're heading right back."

Jessica led Ish out of the cabin, locked up, and hurried to the car. She and Ish climbed in and she locked the doors.

She put the key in the ignition and turned it. Nothing happened.

"Come on, Baby," she said urgently. "Just one more time, I promise!"

She turned the key again. It didn't even try to turn over. No sound, no nothing.

"Please, Baby, please!" she cried. "We have to get home!"

Jessica tried again and again, but the car was silent, refusing to start. She heard the cry come from within herself, a low, gasping sob, but she couldn't give in to panic.

She had to do something. She had to get out of here!

CHAPTER 16

Prodding Ish to hurry, Jessica scrambled back to the cabin with her bag. The only escape now was across the lake. She'd wake up the Whitmans and stay there until she could get help.

She left the lights off at the cabin and locked up again, leaving through the door on the other side of the cabin nearest the lake, and hurried with Ish down toward the dock. She knew the path well, and the full moon, filtering through the birch trees, provided enough light to see where she was going.

Fortunately, her family's motorboat was still tied to the dock. In another week or two, her parents would come up and store the boat in the boat house for the winter. She and Ish climbed in the boat, she unchained it, and pushed off from the dock.

She started the motor and they headed off across the lake. It was cold on the water, and her arms were covered with gooseflesh. She wished she'd brought a jacket.

She knew where the Whitmans' house was. It sat close to the edge of the lake on the far side, but it was so dark, she couldn't see it until they'd nearly arrived there.

She tied the boat at the Whitmans' dock and ran

up to their door. She knocked loudly and called out, "Roger! Marge! It's Jessica! I need help! Wake up!"

She waited a few moments, then yelled and knocked again. There was no stirring from inside the house.

She suddenly had a terrible thought. *Maybe the Whitmans weren't home—maybe they'd left this morning on a trip!* It was only then that Jessica realized she should have phoned them before crossing the lake. She had been so frightened. She wasn't thinking clearly.

Jessica raced around to the drive where Roger always parked his car. It was empty. *The Whitmans weren't home!*

She briefly considered breaking into their house. But she didn't have any tools with her and Roger always locked the shed—where the tools were—when they left town.

Jessica knew she couldn't stay out here all night. It was chilly and getting colder, and the mosquitoes had already found her. She wished she'd stayed back at the cabin. At least there she could stay inside, warm, with the doors and windows locked. And she could call the sheriff in Ryesdale to come out and get her. *Why didn't she think of that before!*

She glanced at her watch. A few minutes after two. Maybe she could get back to the cabin before the caller arrived. *She had to!* There was no other way.

"Come on, Ish," she called urgently. "Run back to the boat! Quick!"

Jessica and Ish scrambled down to the dock and into the boat. She pushed off and they headed back across the lake as fast as the motor would take them.

She and Ish arrived at the dock at 2:11. She tied the boat and ran with Ish back up the slope to the cabin. She didn't hear a car on the lane behind the house and didn't see anyone stirring in the shadows around the cabin. *Maybe they were safe!*

She unlocked the cabin, pushed Ish inside, and slammed and locked the door behind her. She collapsed against the door in the dark, breathing heavily.

"Oh, Ish, we made it!" she said. "We made it!"

Ish wagged her tail, liking the activity and Jessica's voice. She licked Jessica's hand and nuzzled her, asking to be scratched.

"In a minute," Jessica said. "I've got to call the sheriff first." She switched on the light, illuminating the kitchen area.

Her mother had posted emergency numbers on the bulletin board next to the phone. Jessica found the sheriff's number and lifted the receiver to her ear.

She dialed the first number and stopped.

The phone was dead. *Someone had cut the line! He was here! He was already outside the cabin!*

"Oh, my God," Jessica whispered. "Oh, my God."

What could she do?

She needed a weapon. Any kind of weapon.

A gun. No, her dad had sold his hunting rifle two summers ago.

A knife. She rushed to the kitchen drawer. The sharpest knife she could find was a small paring knife. It was better than nothing. She tucked it in her pocket.

It was then that she spotted the baseball bat lying on the floor of the small pantry. She remembered setting it there at the end of her family's last visit. She was supposed to have stored it in the crawl space under the pantry before they left, but she'd forgotten.

She rushed into the pantry and picked up the bat.

If she swung it very hard, she could do a lot of damage.

Holding the bat, she hurried to the door and switched off the light, plunging the cabin into darkness.

I know my way around here, she thought, a lot better than the killer does.

She made her way slowly, groping with her free hand, into the living room and sat in a wooden rocking chair next to the fireplace. Ish lay down at her feet.

She sat—her back rigid, her breathing coming in short gasps—gripping her bat, and waited.

Slowly, her eyes began to adjust to the darkness. The moon, suspended above the large windows, cast a faint silvery glow over the room. Long shadows stretched across the floor toward Jessica, as if reaching for her, to draw her into the shadows forever.

She listened. There was the low hum of insects— mosquitoes mostly, millions of them—buzzing in the darkness outside the cabin, looking for blood.

The quiet was suddenly shattered by the breaking of glass at the back of the cabin. *Someone was coming through the window in her parents' bedroom.*

She rose from her chair and tiptoed into the doorway of the pantry, gripping her bat tightly. Ish followed her, and Jessica nudged her into the pantry and closed the door. She stood just outside the doorway and peered around the corner.

The door to her parents' room creaked as it was opened, and a shadowy figure stepped into the short hall. Jessica raised her bat.

"You know I have to kill you, Jess," the figure said.

The voice so surprised Jessica that she lowered the bat.

The figure stepped into a pool of moonlight.

Talley!

"You?" Jessica cried. "It's *you*, Talley?"

"I didn't want to kill you, Jess," Talley said. "Just those three other girls. But you were getting yourself involved, trying to find out who murdered them—trying to protect good old Kent." Her voice was thick with sarcasm. "I knew you'd figure it out pretty soon."

"But *why*, Talley?" Jessica exclaimed. "Why did you do it?"

"You don't know who I am, do you?" said Talley.

"What do you mean?"

"Remember little Susan Johnson from second grade? Ugly, fat little Susan with the glasses and frizzy hair and no teeth?" Talley said. "Those three girls picked on her unmercifully."

"You?" Jessica cried. "That was *you?*"

"That was me," Talley answered.

Jessica stared at Talley Johnson a moment and it all made sense now. How Talley's hand shook when she looked at the second-grade picture, saying that she didn't like to remember elementary school. How she didn't want Jessica to meet her parents.

"You were afraid your father would say something to me about living here a long time ago, weren't you?" Jessica said. "That's why you never invited me over."

Talley nodded.

"And it was *you* that night at the ravine," Jessica continued. "And you were the one who ransacked my room and took the photograph, weren't you?"

"I didn't want you to look at it too closely," Talley said. "You could have recognized me."

"I wouldn't have known it was you," Jessica said. "You look too different."

Talley laughed loudly. "Thank God for diets, hair straighteners, and contact lenses!" Her face, still half-hidden in shadows, grew serious. "Do you remember when Holly, Carmen, and Monica locked me in the custodian's closet? We were in the second grade."

"I was sick that day," Jessica said.

"I know," said Talley. "I remember as if it were yesterday. We had a sub that Friday, and after recess, they shoved me into that small, dark closet and locked the door. I screamed and cried and pounded on the door—but they just laughed and made fun of me. And they left me there." Talley's voice broke. "I was in the closet, in the dark, for hours—"

"You must have been scared," Jessica said softly. She could understand Talley's fury, even after all these years, but there was a tinge of madness in Talley's voice that reminded Jessica how very dangerous she was.

"I was so terrified," Talley said, "that I peed my pants. And finally, when the sub found me, and I walked out with my jeans wet, the girls laughed all the more. They taunted me about it for the rest of the school year." Talley began to cry. "I was so embarrassed, so humiliated, I vowed I'd get even with them, no matter how long it took."

"So when you moved back here," Jessica said, "you changed your name."

Talley nodded. "Johnson is such a common name," she said, "I knew no one would make the connection. And no one did. So when I registered at school, I told the counselor my name was Talley.

And nobody from the past recognized me, I look so different now.''

"Yes,'' Jessica said sincerely, "you're beautiful now.''

"Not on the inside,'' Talley said. "Inside, I'm just as ugly as I used to be on the outside.'' She sniffled. "I don't have any more self-confidence than I did in second grade. Those girls ruined everything for me.''

"You moved the planchette on the Ouija board?'' Jessica said.

Talley snorted. "Can you believe how stupid Monica was, thinking that a Ouija board could tell her someone was going to die? What a moron!'' She paused a moment. "They deserved to die. I loved watching Monica squirm after I sent her those threatening notes. But she thought they'd come from Kent. I thought Carmen was the idiot, but Monica had to take a close second place. My only regret is that I didn't have time to tell Holly who I was. I mean, what's the purpose of killing someone if they don't know *why* they're going to die!''

"You told Carmen and Monica who you were?'' Jessica asked.

"You should've seen their faces!'' Talley said. "It was worth the nine-year wait, believe me.''

"I'm sorry, Talley,'' Jessica said.

"I know you are,'' said Talley. "You're a good person, Jess. That's why I don't want to kill you. But I have to, don't you see?'' She raised her hand. The gun's metal gleamed in the dim light.

She's going to shoot me! Jessica thought. "But why kill me?'' she said aloud, moving her hand behind her to rest on the pantry door. "We're friends.''

Talley took a step toward her, pointing the gun at her stomach.

"You leave me no choice," she said. "I tried to scare you away by ransacking your room, by leaving the note to warn you—"

Jessica lunged backward and flung the pantry door wide open. Ish came bounding out of the room and joyfully threw herself at Talley, while Jess grabbed for the gun. A shot rang out and Talley staggered backward.

"Talley!" Jessica cried.

"Hold it!" yelled a voice behind Talley.

The hallway was suddenly flooded with light. Jessica put her hands up to shield her eyes from the glare, but she could make out, in that instant, a tall figure standing at the back of the hall.

"Kent!" she cried. "Oh, Kent!"

CHAPTER 17

"So the murders had nothing to do with Holly changing the grades," Jessica said.

"Incredible, isn't it," Kent said. "We were all barking up the wrong tree."

Jessica, Kent, and Tom were sharing a large cheese pizza at Greenwood's Pizazz Pizza Parlor. The smell of cheese and oregano was heavy in the air, and Jessica, sitting next to Kent in their booth, felt relaxed for the first time in over a week.

It was ten o'clock, the night after Jessica had gone to her family's cabin to escape from Holly's and Carmen's killer. The pizza place was nearly deserted and ready to close in a half hour. One of the employees was lazily washing tables.

Jessica's parents were home now. They'd returned immediately after she'd called them from the sheriff's office and explained what had happened. Jess, Kent, and Tom had spent the day at the Greenwood police station, telling their stories separately to Detective Curry.

"Carmen accused Tom of killing Holly," Kent said, pulling up a slice of pizza and looping the string of cheese around his finger. "She came over to my house the other day and told me that Holly'd been blackmailing Tom, threatening to change his grades to all D's if he didn't pay up. That wasn't true, though. Holly was charging kids to improve their grades, but she wasn't blackmailing anyone. She knew it was a simple thing to get transcript 'errors' corrected.''

"That's what you two were arguing about!" said Jessica.

"See," Tom said, "it was my idea to break into the school's grading system." He glanced self-consciously at Kent, who stared back with his mouth set in a grim line. "It was stupid, I know."

Kent didn't respond, but Jessica could feel the tension between the two friends.

"But after I taught Holly how to get into the program, she decided she could benefit from this power," Tom continued. "She had people eating out of her hand—and she bragged that she'd made over three thousand dollars. She charged fifty dollars for every A she entered into the computer, twenty-five for every B."

"So why did she lower your grades?" Jessica asked.

"To be mean—and because I didn't like her new 'business'," said Tom. "All I wanted to do was to change our *own* grades. Just make 'em a little better, you know?"

Jessica smiled. Tom's grades needed more improvement than just "a little." "How are you going to spend your ten-day suspension?" she asked.

"Washing windows," Tom said glumly. "I'm working with the custodians at three schools—after I help the counselors get all the grades changed back to what they're supposed to be."

"When did *you* first find out that Holly was changing grades?" Jessica asked Kent.

Kent took a sip of Coke from his straw. "Last summer," he said. "That's why I broke up with her. It was just so dishonest, and it blew me away that she would get involved in that." He looked at Tom and his jaw tightened. "At the time, I didn't know that Tom was the guy who'd taught her how to do it!"

"I know, I know," Tom said, turning red. "I shouldn't have done it. It was stupid and dishonest."

"How did you find out Tom was involved?" Jessica asked Kent.

"The morning after I walked out on Monica's party," he replied, "she called me. She was really steamed, saying I'd 'ruined' her party. She told me that my 'good friend Tom' was involved with Holly in that grade-changing scheme of hers. At first I couldn't believe Tom would do something so dishonest. But when I confronted him about it, he admitted it had been his idea."

"That's why you didn't want Tom to go to the movie with us?" Jessica asked. "And why you acted so weird that night?"

"Yeah." Kent nodded. "I just felt—well, disappointed in Tom. But I sure didn't think he'd killed Holly! In fact, I never thought that. But with Carmen and then Monica accusing Tom of murder, I was afraid the police would start thinking Tom was responsible."

"Is that why you told me you were with Tom the night Carmen was murdered?" Jessica asked.

"Yeah," Kent said. "I was really at home, doing chemistry homework. But I was afraid Tom would be a suspect. Everyone seemed to know about Holly's 'magic notebook,' and I figured it was just a matter of time before it got around that Holly and

134

Tom had had a big fight about her grade-changing business and that she had demolished his grades.''

Jessica shook her head. "I'm sorry that I ever doubted you, Kent."

Kent took her hand and squeezed. "Jess, I feel so bad about everything you went through. I was so worried about Tom's fate, I was blinded to everyone else's problems. Especially yours."

Jessica returned the squeeze. "That's okay," she said softly. "I understand now, and you had a good reason for acting the way you did." She paused a moment and smiled. "I was so surprised to see you at the cabin last night. And never so glad to see anyone in my life! How did you know I was there?"

"Tom and I pulled into the 7-Eleven just as you were driving out," Kent said. "We got some soda, then decided to drive over to your house. We thought you were heading back home but then we saw the dummy on your front porch and knew you were in trouble. The only place you could've gone driving in that direction was to your cabin. So we drove up there. When we pulled into the drive behind the cabin, we saw Talley's car. And we saw that the back window of the cabin was broken, so we climbed in the way she had."

"When I heard the gun go off, I thought she'd accidentally shot herself when Ish jumped on her," Jessica said. "But it was *your* gun I heard, wasn't it?"

"Yeah," Kent said. "My uncle left me that gun in his will. We stopped home to pick it up before we left for the cabin. I was afraid we might not be in time before—" His voice trailed off. "I'm just so glad you're all right, Jess."

"Me, too." Jessica smiled at him.

135

"So how's Monica?" Tom asked. "Is she going to live?"

"The doctor says she's going to be okay," Jessica answered. "He thinks she'll be back in school in a couple of weeks."

"Tormenting people with renewed enthusiasm, no doubt," Tom remarked.

"Maybe she'll have learned something these last few days," Jessica said.

"Let's hope so," Kent said.

"And what about Talley?" said Tom. "What'll happen to her?"

"Curry says she'll be evaluated by psychiatrists before anything's decided." Jessica sighed. "Poor Talley."

"Yeah," Kent said. "Holly, Monica, and Carmen were terrible to her. Those awful things that happen in childhood really cause deep wounds. I guess some people are too fragile to recover from them."

There was a long silence.

Tom wiped his mouth with a napkin. "Well, that was good pizza. Listen, guys, I'm going to take off. I'll walk home."

"What?" Kent said. "Why?"

"Well," Tom said, "I figure you two deserve a little time to yourselves. Now that you can relax and enjoy each other without worrying about—other things."

"Thanks, buddy," Kent said. "I'll get the check."

"That's another reason I thought I'd split now," Tom said, grinning. "Thanks, Andrews."

Kent laughed as Tom walked out.

"Come on," he said, "let's go for a walk."

"Great," Jessica said with a smile.

Kent paid for the pizza and they strolled out into

the darkness and down the sidewalk. Pizazz Pizza was at the edge of the downtown area just before the neighborhood turned into residential housing. They held hands and walked under the gently humming sodium-vapor streetlights. The air was redolent of freshly cut lawns and autumn leaves.

Jessica breathed deeply. "It smells so good this time of year," she said.

"Yeah," Kent agreed. "It's a beautiful night." He put his arm around her. "I was really worried about you, Jess," he said. "All the way to the cabin, I was thinking about you, seeing your face in my mind. If something had happened to you, I don't know what I would've done."

"I'm just glad you got there when you did," Jessica told him. "I knew Ish would startle Talley and possibly knock her off balance, but I didn't know what I was going to do after that. I had a small knife and a baseball bat, but I don't know if I could've used them on Talley."

"You could've used them if you had to defend yourself."

"Probably. I was scared enough."

"Jess," Kent said, "I've been meaning to explain about my mother."

"What do you mean?"

"You've asked me why she doesn't give me those messages? If she doesn't like you?" Kent said. "Well, it's not that. She—she has a drinking problem. I should've told you this before, but—" He fell silent.

"Hey, that's okay," Jessica said, putting a hand to Kent's cheek. "You don't have to say anymore."

"I wanted you to know," he said. "The way she treated you—it wasn't anything personal. She's finally admitted she needs some help."

"That's wonderful," Jessica said warmly.

Kent stopped in the middle of the sidewalk and kissed Jessica gently. He held her against him for a long moment, and then said in her ear, "You remember the other day in front of the Media Center? Remember what I said to you?"

Jessica nodded.

"I meant it then, and I mean it now," he said softly. "I love you, Jess. I love you very much."

Jessica hugged him tightly. "I love you, too, Kent," she said.

She felt happier than any time she could remember. Things were okay now. She was learning to be independent, to stand on her own without having to rely so much on parents or friends. But that didn't mean she had to be completely alone.

It was time to get on with her life. Something told her it was going to get better and better, and all the trauma of the past weeks would soon begin to fade in her memory. It had been a terrible time, but she had survived, thank God, and grown, and life would go on. Nuzzling into the warmth of Kent's body, something else told her that Kent Andrews was going to be at her side.

She sighed contentedly and kissed him once more. Then they continued their stroll down the sidewalk.